BANSHEE

(THE ROYAL HARLOTS BOOK 1 - A SPIN-OFF FROM THE ROYAL BASTARDS: HUNTSVILLE CHAPTER)

K.L. RAMSEY

HARLOTS

LILIANNA

Lilianna James walked into the bar and looked around. It was the last known address for her older brother, Cillian, but why would he give their mother a bar as his forwarding address? She didn't know very much about her brother, other than her mother missed him terribly right up until her passing and she blamed herself for the time that he did in prison. As if their saint of a mother could be responsible for anything like that. Her mum died believing that nonsense. She said that she felt guilty about leaving Cillian in America and if only she brought him home with them, to Ireland, things would have been different for him. Maybe she was right, but Lili had a feeling that her big brother would have found trouble no matter what country he lived in.

The address that he left as his last known residence was a good indication that her brother hadn't changed a bit since she last saw him. It was a bar, for Christ's sake, called Savage Hell and she was pretty sure that most of the guys in here were fresh out of prison, just like her big brother. The last letter home told the family that Cillian was out of prison and could be reached at this place. Lili just never dreamed that she'd actually have to come all the way to America to find him, but she had no choice. She needed his help and if she was turning to Cillian, it meant she was pretty damn desperate.

She boldly walked up to the bar, ignoring the badass bikers who stared her down. "You're not supposed to be here tonight, honey," the hulk standing behind the bar stared her down and she defiantly shrugged. "Tonight's church and if you know what's good for you, you'll come back tomorrow when we allow barflies like you in."

"Are you the owner?" she asked.

"I'm not," he said, squinting his eyes at her. "Name's Bowie. I'm the owner's husband. You're not from around here, are you?"

Lil rolled her eyes at the big guy. That was the very first thing guys asked her as if she didn't know that she wasn't from the states. "No kidding," she mumbled more to herself than to him. "Is this a gay bar then?" she asked.

"What?" Bowie asked. "Why would you think it's a gay bar?" He looked around as if something was amiss.

"Because you said that this place belongs to your husband," Lil said. "Meaning, you're gay, right? I mean I'm not judging you, I don't give a feck," she shouted over the music that had just started. "Jesus—that's loud," she complained.

Bowie smiled at her and nodded. "I told you—no women tonight. It's church and the guys get a little rowdy. And to answer your question, I'm bisexual—my husband, Savage is too. We have a woman we share between us."

She nodded at him as if she was satisfied with his answer

because, as she just admitted, she didn't give a feck about who the guy was fucking. "Your business," she said.

He smiled and nodded back at her. "So, you from England or something?" he asked.

"You think I'm from fecking England?" she asked.

"Well, your accent sounds English," he said.

"How dare you," she shouted over the music. "I'm not from England and I don't fecking sound English. I'm from—"

"Ireland," a man's voice shouted from behind her. "Lil is from Ireland, and she shouldn't fucking be here." She didn't need to turn around to know who was behind her. His Irish lilt gave him away.

Lil turned to smile up at her big brother. "Cillian," she said. "You're really here?"

Cillian held his arms out wide, "In the flesh, Lil," he said. "Now, how about we get to the point of why you're here?" he asked. "I thought you were back home, in Ireland."

"Why should I stay back there when Da and Ma are both dead and buried?" she challenged. "You got to leave that cac town, why shouldn't I have the same privileges you do?"

"That town wasn't a shit town, Lil," he chided. "It was our home and when I left there, only trouble followed me. You'd be better off back home than here, trust me."

"Trust you?" she challenged. "Why should I go and do a crazy thing like that? You broke Ma's heart, Cillian. You left her to believe that she was the cause of you going to prison and she never got over that."

"Not getting home to see Da or Ma before they passed is my major regret, Lil," Cillian said. "I beat myself up the whole time I was in prison, but I can't change any of that now. All I can do is be there for my wife and kids and be the best husband and father I can be."

"Wife and kids?" Lil repeated.

"Yes," he said. "I'm married and have two kids with another on the way. You should come by and meet the family. Hell, why don't you stay with us?" he asked.

"I can't do that," Lil said.

"Why the feck not?" Cillian growled.

"Because it will put you all in danger and I won't do that to you, no matter how angry I am at you, Cillian," Lil said.

"Danger," the big guy behind her said.

"Jesus," she breathed, "there are more of them, and they keep getting bigger," she muttered to herself.

The huge man with the salt and pepper beard laughed so hard that he garnered a good bit of attention, just what she was trying to avoid. "I'm Savage," he said, holding out his hand to her. She looked it over as if it offended her, finally deciding to shake it.

"Lilianna James," she said.

"As in Cillian's little sister from Ireland?" he asked.

"The one and well, not only, since my ma had a bunch of us kids," Lil said.

"She's the youngest," Cillian offered.

"We met when you were just a baby then," he said. "When your family first came to America. I was a friend of your father's."

"Yeah—she was probably a year or so when we got here," Cillian said.

"Okay, can we stop talking about me as if I weren't here?" she asked.

"I like your sister, Cillian," Bowie said. "I've got to get these guys some beers. It was good to meet you, Lil."

"You too, Bowie," Lil said.

"I'd like to hear more about the danger you are in," Savage said.

"I don't see that it's any of your business," she sassed. Savage threw back his head again and laughed.

"Bowie's right," he said. "I like her too. And it is my business what happens to you, Lil. Cillian is like a younger brother to me and that makes you family. I get involved in all my family member's business. How about we use my office for a little privacy?" he asked. She looked around the bar, wondering if she had made a huge mistake looking for her brother there.

"Just give him a chance, Lil," Cillian asked. "He helped me out when I was in prison. Da trusted him, you should too."

"Fine," she agreed. She needed help and if the big guy wanted to give it, then she'd take whatever he offered.

Lil followed the two men back down a dark hallway to a door with the word, "Office" written on it. "You get lost a lot, Savage?" she asked, nodding to the sign.

"Naw—that's mostly to keep the barflies out of here when they come looking for trouble. My wife, Dallas, didn't want anyone stumbling into my office claiming to be looking for the ladies' room."

Lil smiled and took a seat on the sofa that spanned most of the back wall of his office. "I like the way Dallas thinks," she said. "She sounds like a smart woman."

"She is," he agreed, "hot too." Cillian rolled his eyes and sat on the edge of Savage's desk, while the big guy took a seat behind it. "How about you tell us what this danger is that you claim to be in," Savage ordered.

"It's trouble I had back at home, and I think it followed me here," she said.

"It?" Cillian asked.

"Well, more like, 'He'," she admitted. "You remember Cian Walsh?" she asked.

"Yeah—he was just a kid when I went to prison. I remember Ma telling me how you followed him around like a lovesick puppy," he teased.

"Did not," she grumbled.

"Is he the one putting you in danger?" Savage asked.

Lil sighed, knowing that she might as well start from the beginning if she was going to get it all out. Playing twenty questions wasn't getting her anywhere. "Let me tell it and then, ask your questions," she ordered. Both guys sat back and waited for her to go on with her story.

"Cian got himself mixed up with a bad crowd back at home," she said. "Kind of like you here, Cillian, but he didn't end up in prison. Instead, he pissed off the wrong people, and well, he had to take off for America to keep one step ahead of them. The gang he went up against threatened to kill him and everyone he cared about if they ever crossed paths again. He left Ireland, but he also left someone behind whom he cared about."

"Let me guess—you?" Savage asked.

"Right, but I had no idea that he felt that way about me. I mean, maybe I did have a little crush on him, but he barely spoke to me outside of school and all that. I thought that he didn't even know that I existed until the leader of the gang showed up at my job. I worked for a local doctor, as a receptionist, and I really loved that job. Anyway, this guy—Sid something or other, came in and told me that I was the only link he had to Cian and that I had five days to produce him, or I'd be dead."

"Shit," Cillian grumbled.

"Right," she agreed. "Well, I didn't want to go to any of our siblings back home. They all have families and such, and until a few minutes ago, I had no idea that you were in the same boat. I would have never come here if I had known, Cillian. I'd never want to put your family in peril."

"I believe you, Sis," he said. "But you're here now, so why not let us help you?"

She didn't answer his question, just kept right on with her story as if she hadn't even heard his offer. There would be no way that she'd accept it. Lil wouldn't let her brother help her because that would mean risking his family—her family, and she wouldn't allow that.

"I didn't know who to trust or where to turn for help, so I grabbed my passport, packed my bags, and got on a plane. I flew here hoping to find Cian, but I realized that America is a much bigger place than I'd ever imagined, so I gave up on that fantasy and decided to look you up. I brought Ma's old letters, that you sent home, with me, and they gave this place as your contact address. I had no idea it was a biker bar," she said. "I guess I was clueless about a lot of things," she whispered more to herself.

"Lil," Savage said. "You don't know me. Hell, you don't really know your brother, but I can tell you that coming to us for help was your best idea yet. This is what we do here at the Royal Bastards. My little club is called Savage Hell, and I can promise you that we'll find whoever is after you and your friend, Cian, and give them hell. You won't have to run anymore, not with our help." Hearing Savage's pretty promises made her want to agree to his offer, but she also knew that the people who were after her would stop at nothing to find Cian and if that meant using her and the people that she cared about to do it, they would.

"You'd be putting yourselves and your families at risk by helping me," she said.

"I've already told you that Cillian is my family and that makes you family too, Lil. We take care of our own and there is no way that we'll let that group of thugs from Ireland anywhere near you. But first, I think that we need to track down your friend, Cian."

"How the hell will you do that?" she asked. Her accent was always a little more pronounced when she was pissed off. "He didn't come to America to be found. I'm sure he's found a way to go off-grid and that's exactly what I should do. It will just be safer for everyone that way."

"No fecking way," Cillian growled. "You're staying with me, and Vivian, and I won't take no for an answer. You came to me for help, Lil. Let me help you. Besides, I think it's time for my kids to meet their Auntie Lil."

"You know, it's very unfair of you to use your children against me, Cillian," she grumbled.

"Is that a yes?" he asked.

What other choice did she have? He was right, she had come all this way, and he was her last option, not that she'd tell him that. "Yeah," she agreed. "I'll stay with you."

"Great," Cillian said. He stood and pulled his cell phone from his pocket. "I'll call Viv and let her know to make up the guest room."

"Thank you," she said. "Thank you both," she said, looking over at Savage.

"You're welcome, Lil. Welcome to the family," Savage said. He stood and crossed his tiny office, pulling her up from the sofa and into a bear hug, nearly squeezing the life out of her.

"Savage," she gasped.

"Yeah?" he asked, still holding her in a bear hug.

"I can't breathe," she choked. He laughed and put her back down on the ground.

"Sorry about him," Cillian said, putting his cell phone back into his pocket. "You'll get used to him though. Viv said that she can't wait to meet you. I'm going to head out, man," he said to Savage. "Sorry about church."

"Not a problem," Savage said, slapping her brother on the shoulder. "Family comes first." Lil wondered if they would feel the same way when one of their family members brought trouble straight to their doorstep because she was pretty sure that was what would eventually happen.

CIAN

Cian Walsh woke to the sound of the garbage truck driving by, and he nearly fell off the makeshift cot he had rigged to sleep on. He was exhausted, but that was nothing new for him. He had felt that way since leaving Ireland over two months ago. At least, he thought it was about two months ago since he lost track of days and even hours while living life on the run. And it was his fault that he had to run. He was an idiot—first class and had no one else to blame but himself.

He'd gone and gotten himself involved with the "wrong crowd" as his Ma used to say. His only saving grace was that she and his Da were no longer around to watch him completely feck up his life. He'd heard the rumors, that he was being hunted, and that showing his face again would only get him and everyone he cared about killed. The joke was on them though— there wasn't anyone like that in his life. He only cared about one woman, and she had no idea how he felt—and now, she never would. Telling Lil that he wanted her could never happen now, and even though that felt like a punch to the gut, it was the only way he'd be able to keep her safe. Lilianna deserved at least his protection in all of this, but he left her unwatched in Ireland, hoping that no one else would have picked up on his feelings for her. If anyone from the Dead Rabbits found out that he was in love with Lilianna James, there would be no stopping them from going after her.

That's what the gang called themselves—the Dead Rabbits, after the New York City gang of Irish mobsters who ruled the streets back in the late eighteen hundreds. They thought that they were clever, naming themselves after a gang of Irish prohibitioners, but what they were doing was so much worse. What the Dead Rabbits did in Dublin played a major contribution to the meth problems plaguing his home city.

Cian thought that putting food in his belly and a roof over his head was worth selling his soul to the devil, but he was wrong. When he joined the Dead Rabbits, they assured him that what he'd be doing for them would be on the up and up. They said that he'd be delivering packages of supplies to their vendors, and they made it sound like he'd be working for the postal service. But the job paid a whole lot more than the postal service did and he should have known even then that he was getting into something that he shouldn't. Once he realized that he was essentially running drugs for one of the biggest mob organizations in Ireland, he tried to get out, and that was when he was told that there was only one way to get out—in a body bag. That's when he took off. He'd heard through the grapevine that the Dead Rabbits were looking for him, and their threat to kill him and everyone he cared about if he ever showed his face again in Dublin. That's when he decided that a fresh start in

America might be in order. He got on a plane and never looked back.

He wanted to call back home to a few old friends and ask about Lil, but he also didn't want to give away the fact that she was important to him. Cian knew that doing so would defeat his whole purpose of coming to America to keep her safe, so he didn't give into temptation, as much as he wanted to. He needed to put her in his rearview and forget that he had ever met her.

For now, He wanted to find a job and with little to no work experience, he wasn't sure what he was qualified for. Cian was pretty sure that his skills running illegal drugs might not land him his dream job in America, so he decided to start small. He searched online for hours every day and was even willing to move to a new town to find work, but the task was nearly impossible. Most days, he found himself giving up and just playing video games or screwing around on his social media accounts. He had set up a new account with an alias and he was sure that no one would figure out it was him. He'd used a nickname that Lil had given him when she was just a young girl. She liked to call him "Sleeveless" because he, unfortunately, chose to wear those stupid muscle shirts without sleeves. He thought that it showed off his muscles, but he was fooling himself. They only showcased his scrawny arms and kids made fun of him for wearing those shirts. He couldn't do much about that since he didn't have the money to just purchase new shirts. His mother was dirt poor, trying to raise him, feed him, and keep a roof over his head after his father died. She had her hands full and there was no way that he'd whine about needing new shirts.

He scrolled around on his social media page and when he found a friend request, he leerily opened it. It was from someone named Banshee and he wanted to laugh because that was what he used to call Lil. He used to like to say that she was as loud as a Banshee and would probably drive him mad or deaf with her screeching.

He accepted Banshee's friend request and a private message popped up on the screen. It was from her, and Cian was beginning to wonder just who this Banshee was. "Worried about you," it said. "Get in touch. I've followed you here." He quickly closed the page and turned off his phone, as if the social media site had offended him in some way.

"Who the hell?" he whispered to himself. Had someone followed him from home, or was someone fucking with him, trying to lure him out of hiding? Cian knew that the only way he'd find out was to ask.

He turned his phone back on and opened his page back up, quickly finding the private message. "Who is this?" he asked point-blank. He knew that a response might take hours to days but when he saw the three little bubbles in the comment, he knew that he was about to have his answer.

"Lil." Was all that was typed back. Why the hell would Lil follow him from Ireland?

"Why are you here, Lil?" he asked.

"Because your friend, Sid, came looking for me," she answered.

"Shit," he growled. "He's not my friend," he quickly typed back.

"No shit," she typed. "I gathered that when he threatened to kill me if I didn't turn you over."

"I'm sorry," he typed back.

"Apologize to me in person. We need to meet," she insisted. There was no way that he'd meet up with her. Sid had Dead

Rabbits watching all over the globe. If he met with Lil, it would put them both in danger and he wouldn't allow that.

"No," he typed back. "I won't meet with you. It's just not safe, Lil," he said.

"It's not safe for either of us now, Cian. We need to come up with a plan and Cillian and some friends are willing to help us do that," Lil typed.

"Your older brother?" he asked. Last he heard; Cillian was in prison.

"Yeah, he's out now and has a family. I'm staying with them. Let us help you, Cian," she said. He wanted to tell her that he would let them help but doing so would put them and their families in danger.

"It's just not safe," he insisted. "If we get too many people involved, none of them will be safe."

"Fine," she typed. "Meet with just me then. We're both already in danger, so what can it hurt?"

It could hurt a lot. Hell, it would hurt his heart when she looked at him with judgment in her beautiful eyes. She would look at him like that too—especially when he told her about how he'd gotten himself tied up with the Dead Rabbits.

"Just give me a chance," she begged. He was the one who should be begging her for a chance. He was a fool for thinking that he had gotten away unscathed by all of this. His past was quickly catching up to him in America. Cian just never imagined that it would be in the form of the sexy little hellfire who followed him across the globe.

"Fine," he agreed. "I'll meet with you, but then you will need to steer clear of me, Lil. I'm not any good to be around right now. It'll only bring you more hardship if you stick around."

"I doubt that," she insisted. "But we can talk about all of

that when we are face to face. I'm going to send you an address where I want you to meet me," she said. "You good with that?"

"Sure," he agreed. He just hoped that he didn't have to travel too far because he was just about out of money and a road trip wasn't something he could afford at the moment.

He studied the address and realized that it was just a few towns away from where he currently was. Lil had been so close all this time and he never knew it. "I can be there by nightfall," he said.

"Good," she said. "I'll be waiting. Don't disappoint me, Cian," she ordered. She was always so bossy; he could almost hear the tone in her voice—that one that told him that she meant business and wasn't to be fecked with. He chuckled to himself at the thought of Lil tossing around orders, especially to her older brother who didn't seem to take an order in his life, from anyone.

"See you soon," he said. Cian turned off his cell phone and decided that he needed to get a shower and put on some clean clothing. He could at least do that since he was going to meet with the woman who had stolen his heart back at home and brought it to America with her now.

———

Cian pulled into the back of the parking lot, behind the bar that Lil had him meet her at. What the hell kind of game was she playing, having him meet her at a biker bar? Maybe he had misread the situation and Lil was truly there to only help him and here he was having dirty fantasies about the girl. Yeah— he'd need to figure out if she was with one of the bikers in the bar, or just liked dive biker bars a whole lot more than he anticipated.

He got out of his pick-up and made his way to the front door of the bar. The sign above it said, "Savage Hell" and he wondered just what kind of hell he was walking into. As soon as he walked into the bar, he spotted Lil and God, she still could take his breath away. She had her brother on one side of her and some guy who looked like a hulk, on the other.

"Cian," she breathed, stepping in close so he'd hear her over the loud music. "Come with me," she ordered, taking his hand into her own. Lil wasn't giving him the option to tell her no. He let her pull him back down a dark hallway and into a small office at the back of the bar. Cillian and the hulk followed them and when Lil closed the door behind him, he worried that he had just walked into a trap.

"What's this all about, Lil?" he asked.

"This is Savage," she said, pointing to the hulk who had his arms crossed over his massive chest. He nodded at Cian, and he obliged by nodding back. It was a strange custom that Americans did when they didn't want to shake hands. Almost as if he was being sized up and he was pretty sure that the hulk would find him lacking.

"He owns this place and is the president of the club that meets here. And you remember Cillian?" she asked.

"Good to see you, mate," Cillian said, holding his hand out to him. Cian shook it and stood back, not knowing what the hell to do next.

"You got the introductions out of the way, Lil," he said. "Now, how about you answer my question?"

"Right—what's this all about? Well, we want to help you, Cian," she simply stated. Helping him would end up getting them all killed and while he thought she was sweet for offering; she had no idea what the hell she was getting herself and her friends and family involved in.

"No," he said.

"No?" the hulk questioned.

"Listen, while I appreciate the offer, I can't let you or anyone else get involved in my mess. The Dead Rabbits don't play games and they will kill you and everyone you love if you get involved with helping me." Cian sunk to the sofa in the back corner of the room, suddenly feeling more tired than he had in a damn long time. "They're ruthless."

"I know," Lil almost shouted. "The leader of the Dead Rabbits showed up at my door. His name is Sid and he told me that I either produce you or he'll kill me and everyone that I love. That's how I ended up here. I couldn't lead him to my siblings in Ireland."

"So, you lead him here, to Cillian?" Cian sounded as if he was accusing her of some wrongdoing and that wasn't what he wanted. "I'm sorry, Lil," he whispered. "I didn't mean it that way." She sat down next to him on the sofa and took his hand into her own. She'd never touched him like that before.

"You can't keep running, Cian, and I'm betting that you can't handle the Dead Rabbits on your own. Let them help you," she said, nodding to Savage and Cillian. She was right, he couldn't keep running and now that Lil was involved in his mess, he had to find a way to break free from the Rabbits; if not for his sake, then for hers.

"Fine," he grumbled. "But you can't stay at your brother's— they'll find you there and will kill him."

Cillian barked out his laugh. "I think that I can handle myself," he boasted. "I can take care of Lil and my family."

"Family?" Cian asked. "As in a wife and kids?"

"Yep," Cillian said. "Why?"

"You have to get them out of town," Cian warned. "If the Dead Rabbits don't know about them yet, they will. When they can't find Lil and me, they'll go after your family for answers. The Dead Rabbits have clubs all over America. It's where the organization started. They're even here in Alabama. You have to trust me, Cillian." He didn't miss the look that Cillian shot Savage.

"Ryder will get you all to the safe house. You need to get Viv and the kids out of here—he's right. I'm not related to Lil by blood, and they'll never suspect me. I have a place where these two can lay low for a bit until we can set up a meeting with this Sid guy," Savage said.

"A meeting?" Cian asked. "You're as crazy as you look," he accused.

Savage barked out his laugh. "You have no idea, man," he said. "But my crazy ass is going to make sure that you get out of the Dead Rabbits and that they stop coming for Lil. Everyone good with the plan?" he asked. Cian wasn't sure if he was good with the plan or not, but it was the only one that he had. Trusting others and leaning on them for help wasn't his strong suit, but now that Lil was involved in his mess, he had no other choice.

"I'm good," he mumbled.

LILIANNA

Lil walked into Savage's home and was surprised to find it quiet. From what Cillian had told her, Savage, his husband, Bowie, and their wife, Dallas, had a pile of kids. She remembered growing up with all her brothers and sisters and the noise in the house was sometimes deafening. She could remember her Ma telling them all to be quiet so that she could hear herself think for a minute.

A beautiful blond came out from the back of the house. "Kids are asleep," she whispered, pointing her finger at Savage. "You wake them up, you deal with them." Lil choked out her laugh at how the little blond talked to her husband. "Sorry," she said, turning to face Lil and Cian. "The baby is teething, and I don't get much sleep. I'm cranky and by this point of the day, ready for a break."

"Don't blame you at all," Lil whispered. "I don't have any kids, but I remember my Ma feeling the same way come evening."

"I'm Dallas," she said, holding her hand out.

Lil took it, "Lilianna and this is Cian."

"Good to meet you both. I've made us some dinner and then, Savage will go over the plan about getting you both to the safe house. I've also gotten some things together for you both—extra clothing, food, all that stuff."

"I can't thank you enough, Dallas," Lil said. "You all are very kind to help the both of us like this."

"I've already told you, Lil," Savage said. "You're family."

"Where's Bowie?" Dallas asked.

"He's handling the bar tonight since we have church. One of us had to be there," Savage said.

"I hate it when you guys miss dinner. I'll make him a plate and you can drop it off to him on your way out," she ordered.

"Yes, dear," Savage mumbled. Lil found the whole dynamic of Savage domesticated almost comical. At the bar, he was so in control, and no one dared to question him. But at home, Dallas seemed to be the one in charge. Lil instantly liked the sassy blond.

"I appreciate that," Lil said. "Can I help you get dinner on the table?" she asked.

"Well, I never turn down help," Dallas said. Lil followed her into the kitchen and breathed in the smell of what she assumed to be roasted chicken.

"Wow," she said. "That smells amazing. I haven't had a home-cooked meal in ages."

"We try to eat dinner together every night, but on nights that the club has church, I usually get a night to myself," Dallas said.

"I'm not sure that I understand the whole church thing," Lil admitted. "The night that I showed up at Savage Hell, looking for Cillian, Savage grumbled something about me messing up church."

Dallas giggled, "That sounds about right. Church is the club's meeting. It's where they discuss business and things that need to be talked about—man stuff, according to my husbands. No women allowed—it's a very strict policy." Dallas rolled her eyes and turned to take the tray of chicken out of the oven.

"Well, that seems a bit sexist," Lil mumbled to herself.

"No kidding," Dallas laughed. "The guy's Ol'ladies hate that rule and we usually end up meeting on our own—kind of like our own club."

"Ol'ladies?" Lil asked.

"That's what the bikers call their women. Honestly, that title holds a lot of weight—almost more than a marriage license even," Dallas said.

"What do the women do in their little club meetings?" Lil asked.

"Basically, the same as the guys. They talk about things that they want to do and even about Royal Bastard business. They're the main charter for the Savage Hell club. I guess you could say that we're our own little club all in itself," Dallas said. The idea of starting her own MC had Lil's wheels spinning. She didn't like the thought of not being able to participate in the guy's club. Hell, Savage did just about everything to push her ass out of the bar after she showed up so that the guys could get on with their business.

"Why not make it official then?" she asked Dallas.

"You mean, start our own MC?" she asked.

"Do you ride?" Lil asked. The one thing she hated most about leaving Ireland was having to leave her beloved motorcycle back at home. She had a Harley Street 500 that she had just purchased a few months before she had to leave home. God, she loved that bike.

"I do," Dallas said. "At first, I was scared to death to ride by myself, but the guys got me used to having my own bike, and eventually, I got my license. I don't get to go out as often as I like though—especially with the new baby."

"Well, I'd be happy to sit for you sometime, so you can get out on the road. It would be a shame to let your bike go to waste just because you need a sitter," Lil said.

"I appreciate that," Dallas said. "I take it you ride."

"I do," she admitted. "Well, I used to. I had to leave my bike back in Ireland, so I guess I won't be doing much riding over here."

"You're welcome to use my bike any time you'd like, Lil," Dallas offered.

"Thank you. You know, we should start our own MC," Lil said. "You could be the Prez, just like your husband, and we could even find a charter. What about the Royal Bastards?" she asked.

"Not going to happen," Savage growled from the doorway of the kitchen. "The Bastards don't have women charters," he said.

"I'm sure that's just an oversight," Lil countered. "I mean, maybe they just need a woman to present the idea to them is all," she said. Cillian groaned from the back door. He had let himself in, Vivian just behind him, with their two kids in tow.

"Tell me my sister hasn't gone mad and come up with a crazy scheme to start her own club," he said.

"So, you got the gist of it then," Lil teased, kissing her brother on the cheek, and pulling Viv in for a hug. She picked up her nephew and snuggled him close. "And for the record, I don't think that my idea is mad at all. I think it's quite brilliant," she defended.

"I have to agree with her," Dallas said. "Although I don't have time to be the Prez, I'm sure we'd find a good number of the clubs Ol'ladies who'd love the chance to be a part of our club."

"Oh—I love that idea," Viv said. Cillian shot her a look and she shrugged, "Well, I do. Ever since you made me get my license and own bike, I kind of dream of starting my own club."

"What would you call yourselves?" Cian asked.

"Um, I don't know," Lil said. "I mean, we've just come up with the whole idea, really."

"How about the Harlots?" Dallas asked. "It plays off the whole Bastards thing, don't you think?" Lil loved the name, but this whole club idea would have to wait until they got things under control with the Dead Rabbits.

"I love it," Lil said. "The Royal Harlots would be even better. I think I'm going to be tied up for the next bit and won't be able to join any clubs until I get my life back, you know?" she asked.

"It was fun to think about, at least," Dallas said. "But Savage is right, it probably won't happen." Lil stared Savage down. She loved a good challenge—always had.

"Oh Christ," Cillian grumbled. "I hate it when you get like this Lilianna."

"What's happening here?" Savage asked.

"She feels as though you've challenged her," Cillian said. "And when Lil finds a challenge, she usually takes it up and finds a way to solve it. I think that she might be trying to solve you as we speak."

Savage threw back his head and laughed. He seemed to do that a lot around her. "Good luck trying to figure me out, Lil," he said.

"Yeah," Dallas said, carrying a bowlful of mashed potatoes past her husband. "I've been trying to figure him out for years now and I've got nothing. Let's eat." Everyone filed into the dining room and sat around the big table, passing food, and eating like a big family. It had been some time since Lil had a family meal and having Cillian on one side of her and Cian on the other felt right.

"What's the plan?" Viv asked. Lil liked her sister-in-law. She seemed a perfect match for Cillian—something Lil thought her brother would never be able to find after having to overcome his past.

"We need to leave town for a bit," Cillian said. "I'm sorry, darlin'." He reached for her hand and Viv put hers into his, smiling over at her husband.

"I'm the one who's sorry," Lil said. "If I hadn't shown up here, your family would never be in danger and your lives wouldn't have to be uprooted."

"Not your fault, Lil," Cillian promised.

"He's right," Cian said. "It's my fault. I should have never been gullible enough to believe that the Dead Rabbits had me doing jobs that were on the up and up. I was an idiot and now, I've got you all involved. I'm the one who should be apologizing."

"Shit happens," Cillian said. "I got involved with a gang that I shouldn't have, and it landed me in jail for years. I lost so much time. You were lucky to get out before any of that happened to you, Cian. We'll get through this next part," he promised.

"Cillian's right," Savage said. "You got out and that's all that matters now. We'll find a way to help you make it permanent and keep you all safe in the meantime."

"Thanks, guys," Cian said. "I'm not sure what I would have

done if Lil hadn't reached out. I wasn't going to make it out there on my own."

"That's a rough road," Savage said. "No one should have to go through something like that alone, and now, you won't have to." Cian nodded and Lil reached her hand under the table to find his, linking their fingers. It felt right to touch him, almost like she was right where she was supposed to be—by his side, holding his hand.

Savage cleared his throat, garnering her attention. "As for the plan, one of our members, Ryder, is a pilot. He even has his own plane and will fly Cillian's family to the little beach house that we own on the coast. Ryder will double back here and take the two of you up north, to a cabin that another member has up in Maine. It's cold up there this time of year, so we'll make sure to pack you both some warmer clothes. I'm not sure how long you'll be up there, but we'll plan for the worst-case scenario."

"Which is?" Lil asked.

"Which is that the Dead Rabbits won't meet with us, and you and Cian will have to stay hidden away. I know it won't be ideal, but I'm sure that with time, they'll give up looking for you guys."

"You don't know Sid," Cian mumbled. "He won't ever stop looking for us. I've wronged him and he'll take that personally. Hell, he's already gone after the only person I care for." He squeezed Lil's hand under the table, and she smiled over at him. She had so many questions that she wanted to ask him but now wasn't the time. She'd wait until they were alone and then, she'd hit him with her barrage of questions.

"Let's not get ahead of ourselves," Savage said. "I'll reach out to the Alabama Chapter of the Dead Rabbits and see what I can do—one club Prez to another."

"We appreciate that," Cian said. Hearing him refer to them as a "We" made Lil's heart race. "Are we leaving tonight?" he asked.

"Yes," Savage said. "The sooner the better, so eat up." They all did as ordered and by the time they were finished, Lil had to say her goodbyes to her brother and his family. She hated that she just got them all back into her life and now, she was having to let them go indefinitely.

"I'll be seeing you real soon, little sister," Cillian promised. She nodded and smiled, pasting on her brave face. They both knew that it might be some time before they saw each other again, but she had to stay positive—it's what had gotten her this far.

CIAN

C ian felt enormous guilt that his mistakes were tearing Lil's family apart—especially now that they had all found each other again. Lilianna tried to be brave, smiling and telling him that this little trip to Maine was going to be an adventure, but he could feel her sadness when her brother left. It nearly gutted him.

They hung around Savage's home, waiting for Ryder to get back from flying Cillian's family to the coast. He seemed like a decent guy and when he flew them up to Maine, promising to return to check in on them soon, Cian believed the guy. He was easy to take at his word.

They had been outfitted with warm clothing, food, and everything that they'd need to survive for weeks up at the cabin. They were given new cell phones so that their old ones couldn't be traced, and Savage had Bowie wipe their social media pages out of existence. They were nearly untraceable and that worked for him. Savage had given them strict instructions to stay offline, off-grid, and to only contact him in an emergency. It all should have scared the hell out of him, but all Cian could think about was the fact that he and Lil were finally going to be alone, and he was going to have his chance with her.

Would she want that with him though? He knew that she cared about him. Hell, she had held his hand all through dinner, but that didn't mean that she'd want him the way that he wanted her.

She had been the annoying kid who followed Cian and her older brother, Owen, around like a puppy dog. At first, he thought that she was pretty cute, but as they got older, he began to find her more of a nuisance. By the time he went away to university, he was happy to be rid of his little secret admirer, until he went home on a holiday break. It had been almost two years since he last saw Lil, and she'd grown up. She'd grown up well.

They were at her parent's holiday party, and he wasn't sure if she had even noticed that he was in the room. She didn't so much as look in his direction and God, it was all he wanted— just a bit of her attention. He wished she'd follow him around the old house, asking him a million questions, and begging him to be her boyfriend, just as she had when she was a little kid. Lil was in her last year of Secondary School and all he wanted to do was walk across that room and beg her to be his, like the lovesick puppy she portrayed all those years, but he didn't have the nerve.

Cian had gone back to university and Lil was all he could think about. He wanted her and the only way he could see that happening was if he quit school and moved back to town. He was afraid that Lil would graduate from school and find someone to settle down with, and then, he'd be too late. Cian couldn't let that happen, so he foolishly flunked out of university that semester and went home with his head hung and tail between his legs. Secretly, he was overjoyed to be back and find out that Lil hadn't settled down at all. In fact, she was the wild, crazy spirit that he remembered chasing him around, and that made him fall for her even harder if that was possible.

He'd see her around town and when everyone else was talking about him being a loser for failing out of university, all he could think about was her. He wanted Lil but still hadn't worked up the courage to tell her how he felt about her. So, he followed her around like a love-sick puppy—their roles ironically reversed, until one day, when he literally bumped into her on the road.

She had dropped the books she was carrying home from the library. They were all about chemotherapy and dealing with cancer and he worried that she was sick. She told him about how her mother had found out that she had cancer and as the only kid still living at home, it was her turn to take care of her mother. Lil said that she didn't mind, really, but he could see the pain in her eyes. She was going to have to watch her mother waste away and all Cian wanted to do was be there for her. He had to do the same with his father and the thought of watching Lil suffer through this broke his heart. Cian promised her that he'd stop around to check on her and her Ma and the very next day, he showed up with a pot of his mum's chicken noodle soup. It was in the recipe box she'd left him and one of his favorites.

Cian had moved into his parent's old house and the place felt so cold and empty without either of them still there. They had both passed—first his father and then, his mother, leaving him to fend for himself. Sure, he was an adult, but that was what it felt like to him; them leaving him alone to face the world.

Making a big pot of his mother's chicken noodle soup made the home feel as though it had come to life for the first time in a damn long time. It was the soup that she'd make for him or his father when they were under the weather, and it felt right to be making it for Lil and her mum.

He delivered it to her home and when Lil asked him to join them for supper, he couldn't help but agree. Sitting with her and having supper with her and her Ma felt right, so the next night, he showed up with another one of his mum's favorite meals. Again, she asked him to join them, and this continued for months—until her mother sadly passed from her illness. By that point, he was working for the Dead Rabbits and the idea of telling Lil that he was in over his head with them didn't sit well with him, so he ghosted her. He stopped going around, knowing that she'd need him the most now. He left her without a shoulder to cry on or an ear to listen to her sorrow and that made him feel like a first-class asshole but involving her in his mess wasn't something that he was willing to do.

Now, he'd been given the chance to make everything right with her and that was exactly what he wanted—a chance. He'd just need to convince Lil to give him one, even when he didn't deserve it from her. He just needed a chance to make things right with her.

By the time they got up to the little cabin that they'd be calling home for the near future, he was beat. Lil looked just as wiped out as he felt and poor Ryder looked about ready to drop.

"Will you fly all the way back to Alabama tonight?" Lil asked.

"Yep," Ryder said. "I'll probably grab a few hours of shut-eye and then head back home. My wife is expecting, and I don't like to stay away too long."

"Aww—that's wonderful," Lil said.

"Do you have any kids?" Ryder asked her.

"No," she breathed. "No husband and no kids," she said, looking straight at Cian.

"Don't look at me," he said. "I don't have any kids, or a husband, for that matter," he teased. She giggled and shook her head at him. They got everything unloaded into the cabin and said goodbye to Ryder, leaving him and Lil all alone.

It was suddenly very quiet in the small cabin, and he wasn't sure what to do or say next. Cian wasn't usually at a loss for words, but around Lil, he felt quite tongue-tied. "What should we do now?" she asked, seeming just as nervous as he felt.

"Um, unpack," he said. He sounded more like he was asking than telling her.

"All right," she agreed. "Which room do you want?" Savage had pulled Cian aside to warn him that there was only one bedroom in the cabin. He asked the guy not to tell Lil, worried that if she knew about it ahead of time, she wouldn't agree to even get on the plane.

He winced and she dropped her bag to the hardwood floor. "Tell me that there is more than one bedroom, Cian," she ordered.

"I wish I could, but this place has only one, Lil," he said.

"You knew about this and didn't tell me?" she accused.

"Yes," he said, "but in my defense, I did it for your own good. I knew that if you found out that there was only one bedroom here, you'd put up a fight or not come at all. I needed you to get on that plane so that I'd be able to keep you safe, Lil," he said. It was all he wanted to do now.

"I can keep myself safe," she spat. She could too. That was the thing about Lil—she was the most capable woman that he'd ever met.

"I know that, but I'd like a shot at it too. You're in this trouble because of me, Lil. I just want a chance to redeem myself," he admitted.

"By tricking me into bed with you?" she asked. "That's not exactly a redeemable quality, Cian," she said.

"No," he said, "it's not like that at all. I'd never force you to do anything that you don't want to, Lil. I'll even sleep on the sofa to prove it." She looked him over and shook her head.

"Thanks for the offer, but I saw the sofa and you'll never fit on it. You'll hang over and it will kill your back. We'll figure something out. We'll both need sleep to stay on top of our game," she said.

He wasn't sure if he should even ask this next part. "So, same room then?" he asked.

She nodded her head. "For now," she agreed. "We will see how things go. I'm sure that we can build a pillow fort down the middle of the bed to make sure that you stay on your side." He bit his tongue to keep from telling her that no number of pillows on the bed would keep him from finding her. He had a feeling that he'd be drawn to her no matter the circumstances and Cian would find a way to get to her.

LILIANNA

They spent the rest of the afternoon working in silence. It was killing her that Cian was giving her the silent treatment. He was usually so bubbly and talkative, she'd come to expect him to be gabbing about, but his silence was deafening.

"I'd love to know what you're thinking, Lil," he almost whispered. They had finished unpacking and were working on making something for dinner. She agreed to make the chicken and he was in charge of the veggies. That was the only conversation that they had in over two hours, and it involved poultry and vegetables.

"I'm thinking a lot of different things right now, Cian," she admitted. "Mostly about how we ended up here. I guess I'm wondering why you did it—why'd you join the Dead Rabbits?"

"I just wanted to belong to something, you know?" he asked. "I'd been alone for so long now—no parents, no siblings, and well, I needed something to belong to. I thought that the Dead Rabbits would be that for me, but I was an idiot. I had no idea that I was running drugs, Lil. You have to believe me." She looked him over and saw the young boy she used to follow around when she was just a girl. Lil could see the sincerity in his eyes, and she knew that Cian would never lie to her.

"I believe you," she whispered. She reached up to cup his jaw with her hands. "It just hurt when you stopped coming around after my Ma died. I needed you and you just disappeared from my life," she breathed.

"I was already mixed up with the Rabbits then. I figured out what I was doing with them, and I didn't want my troubles to darken your doorstep. I felt awful not being there for you, Lil. I'm so sorry about your mum, but I didn't feel that I was worthy to be around you. I wasn't any good for you, Lil."

"You're a good man, Cian. You just got involved with the wrong crowd. We can make a fresh start here in America. You got out and that's all that matters," Lil said.

He grabbed her hands into his own and pulled them from his face. "No," he said. "You deserve better than me, Lilliana. You deserve a man who can give you the world, and I have nothing to offer you. I almost got you killed—how can you be so kind to me?" he asked.

"Because I've loved you since I was just a little girl, Cian," she admitted. "And I know you care for me too, otherwise the Dead Rabbits would have never shown up on my doorstep, would they?" She knew that she was issuing him a challenge and there was nothing Cian liked more than a good challenge. If he told her that she was wrong and that he didn't care for her, it would be the first time that he'd ever lied to her.

"I know that you care for me, Cian," she repeated.

"I do," he breathed. "God help me, I do, Lil. I've fallen in love with you too."

She smiled up at him and nodded, satisfied with his answer. "I know," she whispered. "I guess that following you around like a love-sick puppy all those years paid off," she teased.

He barked out his laugh. "You were the most annoying, stubborn girl that I had ever met, Lil," he accused. He was right. Cian was two years older than her and the very last thing that he probably wanted was a young girl following him around like he had hung the stars.

"I have to admit though, I'm damn glad that you follow me around still. I mean, you did come all the way to America to track me down," he said.

"Not completely," she said. "I tried to track you down, sure, but I also wanted to find a way out of Ireland. I was afraid that your old friend, Sid, would make good on his promise to kill me off if I had stuck around."

"I, for one, am glad you didn't stick around to wait for Sid to make good on his threats. He would have, you know?" She nodded. Lil was sure that Sid would have killed her and then she never would have been able to hear Cian admit that he was in love with her.

"I'm just sorry that you had to give up your life in Ireland because of me, Lil," he said.

"I'm not. It was worth traveling to the states to hear you tell me that you're in love with me, Cian," she teased.

"I'm glad that I could make it worth your while then," he said. Lil turned off the flame under the frying pan and moved the chicken to another burner. She crossed the small kitchen and wrapped her arms around his neck.

"So, what do we do next, Cian?" she asked. He pulled her

against his body and all she could think about was the fact that it felt right to be there.

"I've wanted you for so long, Lil. Ever since I flunked out of university to be closer to you," he admitted.

"Wait," she said. "You flunked out of university to be near me?" she questioned. "Why would you do that?"

"Do you remember that Christmas that I came home for the first time in over two years?" he asked.

"I do," she said. "I tried to ignore you the entire evening because I was so mad that you had stayed away for so long. I felt as though you abandoned me, Cian." He dipped his head to gently kiss her lips and she smiled up at him. "That's the first time you kissed me," she whispered.

"Is not," he said. He was standing so close to her; she could feel his warm breath on her cheek. "I kissed you when you were six and I was eight—in the hallway outside of your bedroom," he reminded. She thought back to that day, her hazy memories playing through. She had dared him to kiss her, knowing that her brother's best friend would never back down from a dare, especially from a girl.

"I remember that," she said. "I dared you to kiss me and you were determined not to look like a chicken in front of my brother, so you did."

"I wanted to kiss you, Lil. I thought it was cute the way you followed me around," he admitted.

"Liar," she accused. "You said I was annoying."

He shrugged, "In time, you grew to be very annoying. I guess it became less cute to have your best friend's kid sister following you around while you were in Secondary School. But when I came home that holiday, I couldn't take my eyes off you, Lil. You grew from a nerdy, pestering child into a beautiful woman. I was worried that if I stayed at university after you graduated from school, I'd end up losing you to some wanker who didn't deserve you. I knew then that I was in love with you, but I was a coward and didn't tell you. Maybe things would have been different if I had," he said. "Maybe I would have felt less alone, and I wouldn't have gone and joined the Dead Rabbits."

"We can't live on maybes and what-ifs, Cian," she said. "But we can make the promise to always be honest with each other from here on out," she said. "Deal?"

"Deal," he agreed. Cian pushed her back against the kitchen countertop and she gasped when she felt his impressive erection through his jeans, pressing against her belly. "Tell me if you don't want this, Lil, and we'll stop now."

"I want this, Cian," she whispered. "I want you." That was all he seemed to need to hear from her. He lifted her against his body, helping her to sit on the kitchen counter.

"Here good?" he asked. "I need you and don't want to wait to get to the bedroom."

"Here works for me," she said. He tugged his shirt up his body and pulled it off. He was just as beautiful as she imagined, and so much better than she ever dreamed. Cian's overly long, dark hair spilled around his face as he stared her down.

"Your turn, Lil," he said. She gave him her sassy smile and did exactly as he asked, loving his reaction as she pulled her T-shirt up to reveal that she wasn't wearing a bra. As soon as they got to the cabin earlier, Lil had changed into a t-shirt and leggings. The cabin was warm with just the fire that they had lit in the family room's fireplace.

"Done," she said, tossing her shirt to the floor next to his. "What's next?" she asked. She was hoping that he'd say that touching was next, but he wasn't rushing this, and she wouldn't either.

"Pants," he decided.

"You first," she said, nodding to his lower body. He unbuttoned his jeans and she felt as though she was holding her breath waiting for him to get on with taking his pants down. "Tease," she grumbled. Cian finally got his pants down and now it was her turn to be shocked when she saw that he wasn't wearing under ware.

"Commando?" she asked.

"Yep," he said. "I guess if feel the same way about underwear as you do about a bra."

She giggled and slid to the floor in front of him. "My turn," she said. She shimmied her leggings slowly down her legs and he huffed out his breath.

"Now who's the tease?" he asked.

"Well, I like to give as good as I get," she sassed. She took her time pulling her leggings and panties down her body and when she got them off, she stood and crowded into his space.

"This is fun," she said. "What next?" They were both completely naked, standing in the kitchen, and Lil thought it was probably the most romantic scene she'd ever been a part of.

"You on the pill?" he asked.

"I am," she said.

"I don't have any condoms with me, Lil. I didn't expect any of this, really. If you want to just fool around until I can pick some up in the next few days, we can," he offered.

"Are you clean?" she asked.

"I am," he agreed.

"I am, too," she admitted. "And I'm good with my birth control, Cian. I trust you." He lifted her against his body as if that was all he needed to hear from her. He walked back to the bedroom and dropped her to the mattress, causing her to giggle.

"So eager," she teased.

"More than you'll ever know," he whispered. "I've waited a damn long time for this, Lil. I've waited a long time for you."

"Same here," she said. He covered her body with his own and she felt completely blanketed by his love. She wrapped her arms and legs around him, pulling him closer. "I love you so much," he whispered. Cian brushed his lips over hers and ignited the same electrical sparks she felt a few minutes ago when he kissed her in the kitchen.

"I love you too," she breathed. He ran his cock through her drenched folds and Lil moaned. "You feel so good," she groaned. "Please, Cian." He thrust into her body and moaned out her name. It felt so right to have him inside of her. With every thrust, she became his, and with every kiss and caress, she lost another piece of her heart to him.

"You're mine, Lil," he whispered.

"I've always been yours, Cian," she promised. "Always."

He fucked her until she was screaming out his name and when she didn't think she'd be able to take another second, he found his release, calling out her name. Cian held her against his body, pressing hers into the mattress, as he softly kissed her. It was perfect. It was more than perfect—being with Cian was everything that she'd ever dreamed it would be and so much more.

"Mine," he whispered, rolling off her. He pulled her against his body and held her as she drifted off to sleep. For the first time since leaving Ireland, she felt as though she had found her home. It was Cian—he was her home, her heart, her everything.

It had been two months of them being tucked away in their little cabin up in Maine. It was everything she ever dreamed it would be—living with Cian. Every day that passed, she loved him more. They'd sit up at night on the front porch of the cabin, wrapped in quilts, looking at the stars, and reminiscing about their shared childhoods. If she could go back and tell her younger self that someday, she would have ended up with the man of her dreams, she would.

Lil had spent so many nights crying herself to sleep because Cian didn't seem to even notice her. She had loved him for so long, she couldn't believe her luck of finally landing him. Lil wanted to tell him to pinch her, just so that she'd know that he wasn't a dream, but she didn't want to sound like a love-sick sap.

Cian, on the other hand, seemed to be going crazy being trapped at their cabin with her. He assured her that he was fine, but she could see that he was going stir-crazy being cooped up in Maine. She found him in the kitchen, making them their morning coffee, and wrapped her arms around him from behind.

"Sleep well?" he asked.

"Yes, you?" She felt him shrug and smiled to herself. "If I remember correctly, you used to be a runner."

"Sure, back when I was young and fit," he teased.

"Um, I've seen you naked, Cian. You're still pretty damn fit. As for young, you're only two years older than I am, so watch calling me old." He laughed and turned, pulling her into his arms.

"What's your point, Lil?" he asked.

"Why not go for a run?" she asked. "I mean, we've been here for two months now and haven't left this cabin." Savage had their groceries delivered, along with everything else that they needed, so there was no reason for them to leave the cabin. Well, except to keep their sanity.

"Just go for a run," she ordered. "I'd love for you to get some fresh air and maybe even come back less of a sourpuss," she teased.

He grimaced and nodded. "You sure that you'll be okay here for about an hour? It will be the first time that we're apart in two months."

"I'm sure," she said. "Besides, some time alone might be good for us. I'm planning on taking a nice long hot bath while you're gone."

Cian chuckled and nodded, "Fair enough," he said. "Maybe I'll even join you when I get back from my run."

Lil wrinkled up her nose and shook her head. "I'll be squeaky clean by then and you'll be a sweaty mess. I think you should shower first. How about I meet you in the shower when you get back?" she asked.

"It's a date. I'm looking forward to messing you up again after your bubble bath," he joked. He kissed her and swatted her ass on his way back to the bedroom. "See you soon, darlin'," he promised.

CIAN

He'd run until his legs felt like they were turning to jello and then, he ran a few more miles before turning back to run to the cabin. All in all, he felt a hell of a lot better and although he hated to admit it, Lil was right. Leaving the cabin and going for a run was a good idea. He was starting to feel more like himself and that hadn't happened since he had left Ireland.

He ran about five miles back to the cabin before he noticed the billow of smoke coming from that direction. "Shit," he mumbled to himself. His legs, which moments ago felt as though they couldn't run another mile, suddenly got a second wind and he ran back to the cabin. And what he found stopped him cold. The cabin was on fire and there was almost nothing left of it or his pick-up truck.

"Lil," he screamed at the burning cabin. If she was still in there, she wouldn't be alive. He dropped to his knees. Cian had lost his entire world and he only had himself to blame. Lil was gone and this was all his fault.

"Sid," he shouted, standing, and turning in a circle, hoping to find the fecker there. He knew that the guy had to have done this. Sid had taken his whole world from him and now, he had nothing more to lose. He needed to find that asshole and then, he'd find a way to avenge his Lil. He found a white piece of paper nailed to a tree that stood next to the cabin. It was the only thing not on fire in the vicinity and he knew that it had to be left behind for him to find. Cian walked across the yard and read the note, holding it taught so that it wouldn't flap in the wind, the smoke almost choking him.

"I have her," he read out loud. "You want her back, you come find her." It was crazy to feel so much relief about the fact that Sid had Lil. Knowing that she was still alive, for now, was enough for him. He pulled out his cell phone and took a picture of the note, with the address on it, just as the tree's branches caught fire.

"I'm coming, Lil," he whispered, tucking his cell back into his sweats. He started for the main road. First, he needed to find a rental car, then, he'd drive back to the address in Huntsville, Alabama that Sid had left for him to find. He'd follow the trail left for him if it meant finding his woman. There'd be nothing to stop him from getting to Lil—not even Sid and the Dead Rabbits.

He sat in the rental car, just outside of the Alabama warehouse where Sid told him to meet him. Cian wasn't a fool—if he walked into that warehouse, they would kill both him and Lil. There was no way that Sid would let either of them live, knowing what they knew about him and the Dead Rabbits. Lil had done enough research to bring down Sid while they were in the safehouse, but they still couldn't go to the authorities for fear that they'd be in Sid's pocket. Back in Ireland, the Dead Rabbits owned the cops, and he was sure that the same would hold true in America. Sid would leave no stone unturned to get what he wanted, and Cian had a sick feeling that what he wanted was both him and Lil dead.

He sat in that fucking car for almost two days, watching the change of guards, counting the men who went in and came out of the warehouse. He needed intel if he was going to go to Cillian and Savage to ask for their help. That was the plan, asking Lil's brother and his club to help him get her back because there was no way that he'd be able to live without her. She had become his whole world since she found him in America and there was no way that he'd let Sid or anyone else take her away from him.

He had counted about twelve guards. He also knew that Sid was coming and going from the warehouse, and he might be in there when they finally formulated a plan to go in for Lil. That would make thirteen and he knew that he wouldn't be able to handle those odds on his own, even if his mind was playing tricks on him from lack of sleep, telling him that he could take them all. Sleep deprivation had him believing that he was invincible and that would only end up getting Lil killed.

After two days of laying low, pissing in the woods, eating protein bars, and praying that they'd transport Lil to give him the chance to grab her, he decided that it was time for him to call Cillian.

Cian went to the only hotel with a vacancy in Huntsville and booked a room for the night. He showered, shaved, and changed into some new clothes that he had picked up. It was time to schedule a meeting with Cillian and come up with a good plan to get Lil back, hopefully, one that would end up with them both alive and Sid behind bars.

He pulled the burner phone, that he bought at a gas station, from his pocket and dialed Cillian's number, thankful that he had committed it to memory. "Who the feck is this?" Cillian answered.

Cian barked out his laugh. "Is that really how you answer the phone?" he taunted.

"When I don't know who's calling, sure," he growled. "So, I'll ask you again—who the feck is this?"

"It's Cian," he said. "Listen, Sid got Lil and I want her back. You in for helping me?"

"Shit, Cian," Cillian growled. "You need to give me some more details. How the hell did Sid get my sister?"

"I went out for a run, and I got back to the cabin and found it and my truck both blown to bits. I thought she was dead until I found a note nailed to a tree in the front yard. Sid left me a message and told me where I could find her. He wants me to trade myself for her," Cian said.

"And you don't trust his offer, right?" Cillian asked.

"Not a bit," Cian admitted. "I know that if I walk into the warehouse where he's holding her, we'll both end up dead. I need a plan and some manpower, Cillian. You in?" he asked again.

"Of course," Cillian agreed. "I'll do whatever it takes to save my sister, Cian."

"We're going to need some of your club members," Cian said. "They have a small army guarding her."

"Is she local?" Cillian asked.

"In a warehouse on Monroe Street, in Huntsville. But before you go and get the idea to play hero—he's got about a dozen guys there guarding the building. They are heavily armed, and the place is locked up like a prison. Getting in will be tricky enough without you going and playing Lil's savior."

"Understood," Cillian agreed. "Plus, Viv would kick my ass if I went in there alone to get myself killed. I'm not the same kid I used to be, man." Cian had heard rumors about Cillian when they were just teenagers. Cillian was a few years older than he was, but he'd get all the news from Cillian's younger brother, Declan. They were best friends growing up and Declan looked up to his older brother until he found himself in hot water back in America.

"Do you think a few of your friends might help us?" Cian asked. If they didn't get enough manpower, there would be no way that he and Cillian would be able to go into that warehouse after Lil.

"I know that they will," Cillian promised. "How about you meet us at Savage Hell tonight?" he asked. "That will give me enough time to round up some help and fill Savage in."

"Thanks, man," Cian said. "I appreciate it. I'm sorry that I let this happen, Cillian."

"You didn't let it happen. Sid took my sister, and we'll get her back—end of story, Cian."

"Thanks for saying that, Cillian," Cian said.

"No problem. Meet us tonight at the bar—seven o'clock, and don't be late," Cillian ordered.

"Got it," Cian said. "Thanks." He ended the call and laid down on the king-size bed that took up most of the hotel room. He had about six hours before he'd have to head over to Savage

Hell and that gave him enough time to grab a few hours of shut-eye.

Cian walked into Savage Hell and turned to find the bar full of women. "What's all this?" he asked. Savage walked out from behind the bar and Cillian flanked his side.

"The women insisted on being here for this meeting. You see, my sister has sparked an idea to start a sister chapter of the Royal Bastards in our area, and well, as you can see it's caught on."

"We're going to get Lil back and then, we'll convince her to be our Prez," Dallas said. "The Royal Harlots need her, and we won't let that fucker, Sid, take her from any of us."

"I appreciate that, Dallas," Cian said. "But you have no idea who you're going up against."

"I think we do," Vivian said. She was Cillian's feisty wife and if she could put up with her husband, Cian was sure she could handle a few Dead Rabbits. "You see, I've done a little bit of research and well, Sid's here without a visa. The Department of Homeland Security is very interested in Sid being here in Alabama and has even offered to help us track him down."

"Really?" Cian asked. "You're one lucky son of-a-bitch, Cillian," he said. "I've been looking for a loophole to get Sid sent back to Ireland for weeks now and your wife did it in what—days?" he asked. She nodded and Cillian laughed.

"You don't have to tell me how lucky I am, Cian. Viv is a bloody genius. Now, how about we get my sister back? I'm sure she's probably sick of waiting around for one of us to show up and sooner or later, she'll take matters into her own hands."

"That might not end well for her," Savage said.

"Hell, I'd lay money on it not ending well for Sid," Cian said. "But yeah, I want her back. You have to know that I plan on marrying your sister once we have her back, Cillian." He wasn't asking her brother for permission, more like telling him what his plans were once he got his woman back. That's what she had become over the last two months of hiding out at the cabin up in Maine—his.

"You asking or telling?" Cillian asked, crossing his arms over his chest.

"Bit of both," Cian said. "I love her," he said. The women around the bar all made an "Aww" sound and he groaned. Sure, he sounded like a love-sick sap, but he didn't care.

"Well, if she feels the same way about you, I won't stand in your way, Cian. I'll welcome you into the family with open arms. But the decision is ultimately my sister's, and we'll need to get her back to hear her verdict," Cillian said.

"Agreed," Cian breathed.

"So, what do we know about where she's being held?" Savage asked. Dallas stood and crossed the bar to stand next to her husband, waiting him out for his answer.

"It's a warehouse in town here, actually. It's why I've come back to Alabama, to be closer to Lil. I know where he's holding her, getting into her is another matter."

"How many guards does he have in place?" Cillian asked.

"I counted twelve," Cian answered. "I ran surveillance for almost forty-eight hours, counting men every time there was a guard change. I was hoping that they'd move Lil and I'd be able to get to her, but that never happened. I just couldn't go storming in there with those odds stacked against me. They'd kill us both."

"Agreed," Dallas said. "How about you let us help you? I know you told Cillian that you needed manpower, but don't underestimate our little group," she said. "I'm betting some good, old fashion woman power might be just what you need to distract those twelve or so guards." Dallas looked at Vivian and smiled.

"I've also taken the liberty of checking into what the Dead Rabbit's business is here in Alabama. Apparently, they're trafficking women over the border in Mexico and bringing them up the coast to Huntsville."

"Human trafficking?" Cian asked.

"Yep," Dallas said. "And I'm also betting that if one of the guys shows up with a few of us women in tow, we'll be enough of a distraction for you to get in with Savage and Cillian and get Lil back. Then, we'll let the Department of Homeland Security know where Sid is, and they can take it from there."

Cian nodded, "That sounds like a really good idea," he said. As far as plans went, it wasn't a bad one.

"I'm not crazy about this idea," Savage grumbled, pulling his wife up against his body. "But my wife has explained to me that I have no choice in the matter. She wants to get Lil back to help her start the Royal Harlots, so I'm game."

"I also hate this plan, but Viv has also informed me that I too have no choice. So, I'm going to be the one to bring them in. I've got an Irish accent that won't give away who I am. The only other person who sounds like the rest of the Dead Rabbits is you, Cian, and you can't go in there. You said it yourself—they'll kill both you and Lil. I say you hang back and let the rest of us do this for you. My sister will have my balls if she thinks that I got you killed."

Cian hated the idea of sitting back and waiting for them to

come out the other side of this mess, but what other choice did he have? "Fine," he grumbled. "But I want to add that I am not a fan of this rescue plan either."

"Great," Dallas said. "The guys all hate our plan, so we're on the right track," she teased. She went up on her tiptoes and gently kissed her giant husband's cheek.

"Joke all you want," Savage growled. "If this thing goes sideways, there aren't enough men in Sid's little army to keep me from getting to you." Cian tried not to take Savage's proclamation as a slight, be he had. He hated that he couldn't go in there and pull her out of that warehouse himself, but he couldn't. For now, he'd have to rely on Cillian and his motley crew if he wanted his woman back—and that was the only thing he could think about right now. Getting Lil back was the only thing that mattered to him.

LILIANNA

She had been locked in that tiny, fecking cell for almost three days now and she felt about ready to lose her mind. Sid had only been by once, but she hadn't seen him for the last two days. He had his guards bringing her food, taking her to the bathroom, and even offering her a shower and a change of clothing.

The warehouse that they were holding her in was in Alabama, that much she was sure of. The faded company logo on the back wall of the building was familiar to her. She had seen it when she first got to town, looking for her brother. That seemed ages ago now, but it had only been a few months—a few blissful months of being tucked away with Cian up at that beautiful little cabin in Maine. That was gone now—the cabin, Cian's truck, everything except for her memories. And her hope. She still had that, foolish as it was, but it was there, in the back of her mind. Lil knew that sooner or later; Cian would find Cillian and tell him about her abduction. She didn't know her brother the way she used to, but the one thing she knew about him and Cian—they wouldn't let Sid get away with taking her. The question remained—where were they?

After she had convinced Cian to leave for a run, she ran herself a bath and sunk into it. That's when she heard the noise down in the kitchen and called out for Cian. He didn't answer her, and she knew that something was wrong. Lil wasted no time getting out of her bubble bath and pulling on her pajamas. She needed to find out who had gotten into her cabin, although, she had a pretty good idea—Sid. Or, one of his lackeys. Either way, there was no way that she'd let them take her—not without a fight.

She found Sid sitting at her kitchen table as if he was waiting for her to come down from the bathroom. "Have a nice bath?" he asked. She wanted to tell him to go fuck himself, but that would only give him some sick pleasure. She had known men like Sid before. Hell, she had already had a run-in with him back in Ireland. He wasn't sitting in her kitchen, paying her a social visit. He was there to do exactly what he had promised her he would if she didn't deliver Cian. She just hoped like hell that her guy had gone for a long run. The last thing she needed was to have him walk into the cabin while Sid was there looking for him.

"What the feck are you doing here?" she questioned.

He made a tisking noise and shook his head at her as if he was disappointed in her question. "I'm here to fulfill my promise, Lilianna," he said. "You shouldn't have run. As you can see, I have resources that tracked you down. Now, I'm not going to be so kind in my treatment of you, Lil."

"Just tell me what you came all this way to say, and get the feck out of my cabin," she ordered.

Sid's laughter filled the small space and he nodded to one of the guys who stood in the shadows behind her. Lil knew that they were there, but she had no idea how many there were. Before she could scream for help, one of Sid's men covered her mouth and nose with a cloth that smelled like chloroform. It didn't take long for her world to go dark and that was the last thing she remembered before waking up in this Godforsaken cell.

"I'd love to know what you're thinking, princess," one of the guards taunted her from outside of her cage.

"I'm thinking that when I get out of here, I'm going to fecking kill you," she sassed. He threw back his head and laughed, the sound vibrating off the wall and empty cages that surrounded her. She knew from the stench that the warehouse must have been used in holding humans and that thought made her sick.

"So, human trafficking?" she asked as if they were just two old friends having a conversation.

"You poke your nose in other people's business and you'll end up getting yourself killed, princess," he said. Now it was her turn to laugh.

"Go on then," she taunted. "Do it—kill me." The guard pointed the end of his gun into between the bars of her cage and Lil held her breath waiting for him to pull the trigger and end her misery. She thought about closing her eyes, so she wouldn't see death coming, but that would make her a coward, and Lil wasn't a coward by any sense of the word.

"You've got more balls than most men I know," the guard

said. He sounded almost proud of her and that made her feel a bit queasy.

"Don't underestimate my willingness to die for the person I love. Sid wants me to help you lure Cian here, and I won't do it. So, you might as well kill me now because I refuse to cooperate."

"You have no choice in the matter, princess," the guard taunted. "I like your determination, though. It's been a while since I met anyone with as much spunk as you've got, darlin'." He walked away from her cell, back to the front of the ware- house and Lil knew that shouting after him would only give him the satisfaction that he wanted. He liked to watch her squirm and beg. That's what she had done for the past few days, but no more. Lil was done with all that shit and now, she was ready to give them a fight, because there was no way that she'd let them get to Cian. They'd have to do so over her cold, dead body—that was the only way she'd cooperate with the Dead Rabbits.

Lil woke to the explosion of gunfire all around her and quickly scooted off her cot and onto the concrete floor. There was no way that she'd let them take her out of that cage without a fight. If she was a betting woman, she would have guessed that her rescue squad had arrived. She watched as the guards scrambled around her and when Dallas appeared at her cage, keys in hand, ready to free her, she had to admit, she was a bit shocked.

"You," Lil breathed. "What the hell are you doing here?"

"Rescuing your ass," Dallas said, smiling at her. "You want to get out of here, or is the food that good?"

Lil laughed, "Food's fecking awful," she said. "Get me the hell out of this cage," she ordered. Dallas seemed to hesitate, and Lil's frustrated growl filled the warehouse. "What's the hold-up?" she asked.

"I need your promise that you'll be our leader," Dallas said.

"Leader of what?" Lil shouted.

"Of the Royal Harlots," Dallas shouted back. "A few of the women and I have decided that we like your idea. Savage has gotten in touch with the Royal Bastards and they're willing to charter our sister club, we just need a Prez. How about it?"

"If it means you let me out of the cage, I'll agree to be the fecking Queen of England," Lil growled.

"Mean it, Lil. If you agree to be the Harlot's Prez, then you're really in." Dallas waited her out and when she finally nodded her agreement, Dallas put the key into the lock and turned it, opening her cage.

"Thanks, Dallas," she breathed.

"Come on, Lil," Dallas said. "Our new club members are helping to hold the line while I get you out of here. It's time to fuck up some Dead Rabbits."

"Sid's not here," Lil said.

"Oh—don't you worry about Sid. Cillian, Cian, and Savage have him and they're having a little chat with him. I'm sure that he won't be bothering you or Cian ever again once they get done with him." Lil's smile felt mean. She was sure that they would convince the Dead Rabbit's leader to leave her and Cian alone—otherwise, they'd kill him.

"They're offering him his life for ours, aren't they?" Lil asked.

"Now you're getting it." Dallas handed her a gun and nodded

to the front door. "You ready?" She was more than ready to get the hell out of that place.

"Ready," Lil agreed.

"Then lead the way, Prez," Dallas insisted.

CIAN

They had Sid tied to a chair with bungee cords and every time the fecker moved, he'd bounce back against the wooden chair. It was almost comical to watch Sid thrashing around. He deserved so much more than being bungee corded to a wooden chair for what he had done to him and Lil.

"Let me go," Sid shouted as he thrashed about.

"In due time," Cillian said. "First, we need to get a few things straight. You see, as we speak, our women are taking back what belongs to us. You took my little sister, fecker, and I don't take that lightly."

"Who the hell do you think you are, talking to me like that?" Sid shouted at Cillian.

"I'm a member of the Royal Bastards—you hear of them?" Cillian asked.

"Shit," Sid grumbled. "Yeah—I've heard of them."

"Good," Savage said, seeming to take over the conversation.

"Then I won't have to tell you what will happen to you if you come after one of ours again," Savage said. "You see, Lil is more than one of ours—she's the Prez of the Royal Harlots, and they happen to be our sister club in the Royal Bastards. You chose to fuck with the wrong people, man," Savage taunted.

"No harm, no foul," Sid said. "You said that your women went into my warehouse to get Lil out—so we're good then." Cian wanted to punch the smug smirk off Sid's face, but he knew better.

"No," Cillian shouted. "We're not good. We need your word, as the leader of the Dead Rabbits, that you'll not only leave town, but you'll leave Cian and Lilianna alone."

"I have business in Huntsville," Sid challenged.

"I don't get a fuck," Savage shouted. "You take your organization and your business, and you leave town."

"Or what?" Sid spat.

"Or we kill you—right here, right now. I don't have a problem with that option," Cillian said. "I mean, I've already done time and all. Plus, we wouldn't have to worry about him coming back around."

"That works for me," Cian said. "This fecker destroyed my life and I'm ready to stop running."

"What's it going to be, asshole?" Savage asked. "Your life or your promise to leave town and not come back looking for Cian or Lil?" Savage pulled his gun from his hip holster, to help prove his conviction to uphold his promise.

Sid didn't look very happy about his options, but Cian didn't give a feck. "Fine," Sid shouted. "I'll take your deal. I won't be coming back to this God-forsaken town ever again and Cian and his woman won't be on my radar."

Savage looked at Cian as if to ask if he was good, and he nodded. "Works for me," Cian said.

"Good enough," Savage said. "Take his ass to the airport and put him on a plane back to Ireland," he ordered.

Cillian untied Sid and pulled him from the chair. "Let's go asshole," he said to Sid. "You coming?" he asked Cian.

"No," Cian said. "I'm going back to the bar to meet Lil when she gets back. We have a lot to talk about." Cillian nodded and led Sid out.

"What now?" Cian asked Savage.

"Now, comes the second part of the plan. Good old Sid there is wanted by Homeland Security for being in America without a visa."

"You'd think with everything that asshole's done, they'd be able to get him on more than not having a visa," Cian said.

"I know, but we at least have that much going for us. They'll make sure that Sid goes back to Ireland and stays there. You and Lil will be safe because we both know that fucker won't keep his word. Once Homeland Security gets involved, he'll have no choice but to keep his promises to us."

"Smart," Cian said. "What you said about Lil—her being the Prez of the Royal Harlots, is that true?" he asked.

"Yep, as long as she agreed to be. Dallas was going to spring it on her after they got her out, and knowing my woman, she can be pretty persuasive. I'm betting that she even made Lil agree to take the job as a condition to secure her freedom."

"That's pretty ruthless," Cian said.

"That's my girl," Savage proudly boasted. "Let's get back to Savage Hell—I need a beer."

"Same, man," Cian said. He could use a few beers but first, he needed to hold his woman and ask her to marry him. He was done waiting for the right time to start his life with her. One thing he had learned over the past year, there would never be a right time, he just had to make it the right time to ask Lil to spend the rest of their tomorrows together.

They got back to the bar and as soon as they walked through the front doors, Lil cried out his name, ran across the bar, and jumped into Cian's arms. God, it felt good to be holding her again. It had only been three days, but not having Lil with him made it feel as if they had spent years apart.

"You okay, honey?" Cian whispered into the crook of her neck. She snuggled into his body, wrapping her arms around his neck just a little tighter.

"I am now," she stuttered. "It was awful," she whispered. "He kept me in a cage."

Cian suddenly wished that they had killed the fecker for what he had done to Lil, but at least he had the peace of mind knowing that he'd never be able to get to them again.

"It's over now, baby," he promised. "Sid won't be able to touch either of us again. We're free."

"Really?" she asked.

"Yes, I promise." He turned back to Savage who was holding Dallas between his and Bowie's big bodies. "Can we use your office?" he asked.

"I can do you one better. We have apartments above the bar and you, and Lil can use one for as long as you need until you can get back on your feet," he said. Savage handed him a key and he nodded his thanks.

"Thank you, Savage," Lil said. "I'll need to talk to you about the Harlots meeting here until we can get our own clubhouse," she insisted.

Savage laughed, "Being held captive has made you no less bossy, Lil," he teased. "And my bar is your bar," he offered. "Go get some rest."

"Thanks," she said. She nodded to Cian, and he carried her up the back stairwell to the apartment that they'd be calling home until he could find them something better. He would too. He wanted to give Lil the world, but that would depend on one thing—her saying yes.

He unlocked the door and carried her into the small apartment. It had all the comforts of home—a small kitchen and furnished living room area, and a bedroom. He carried her back to the bed and gently sat down with her, keeping Lil close.

"I need a shower," she said. "I'd like to wash the past few days off of me."

"We'll get to that. For now, I'd like to ask you something," Cian said.

"All right," she said. Lil stayed snuggled into his body. "Ask away."

"Will you marry me?" he questioned. She looked up at him and smiled, taking his breath away.

"Marry you?" she breathed. "We've just been through hell and back. Do you really think that now's the right time to ask me that?"

"Yes," he said. "Now is the perfect time to ask you to marry me. I almost lost you. Hell, I thought that I had when I came back from my run and found that cabin and my truck blown to bits. My whole world collapsed when I thought you weren't in it anymore, but then, I found that damn note Sid left, and it gave me hope. I knew then and there that if I was lucky enough to get you back, I'd ask you to marry me right away. I need you to promise to spend every day with me from here on out," he insisted. "I love you. Say yes, Lil."

"I'd love to marry you, Cian," she whispered. "I love you too —so much." He wiped the tears from her cheeks and dipped his head to gently kiss her lips.

"Thank you, Lil." He felt like the luckiest man on the planet, and he was.

"One condition," she said, holding up her hand. "I've agreed to be the Prez of the Royal Harlots, and I'd like to stick around here. If you're all right with all of that, I'll marry you."

"Already putting conditions on our union," he teased. "I think it's great that you've agreed to be the club's Prez. In fact, I think you'll be a fierce leader—just what the Harlots will need. You'll be their Banshee."

"Banshee," she said. "I almost forgot about the nickname you gave me. I think it will make a perfect biker name, don't you?"

"It's fitting," Cian agreed. "The Bastards will never know what hit them," he teased. She giggled and pulled him down for a kiss. He'd finally found everything he ever wanted wrapped up in one sexy hellcat. His Lilianna—his Banshee.

The End

I hope that you loved Lilianna and Cian's story! Here is a sneak peek at book 2 of K.L. Ramsey's Royal Harlots Series— Danger is coming soon!

DECLAN

Declan James wasn't sure if heading to America was a good idea or not, but he had no other choice. The Dead Rabbits had a bounty on anyone's head related to his little sister, Lilianna. From what he had gathered, she was now going by the name, Banshee, and was the leader of an all-women biker club called the Royal Harlots. That much he had picked up while one of the Dead Rabbits beat the shit out of him, asking where his sister was. Even if he knew where she was, there was no way that Declan would give them what they were after.

He stepped into the bar that his brother Cillian left as his new address in America after the rest of the family had moved back to Ireland. Declan remembered that place, though he was never really allowed in the main barroom, since he was only a kid. His father had met a man named Savage there a few times. He was helping their family to find housing and even tried helping Cillian when they all decided to move back home to

Ireland, although his brother seemed to prove too rowdy even for the big, barley biker who promised to watch over him.

Declan heard Cillian before he spotted him. His older brother still had the same loud laugh that seemed to make the whole building shake. "Cillian," he said, from across the barroom. His brother turned to look him over and Declan could see exactly when his big brother recognized him. Cillian hadn't seen him since he was just a kid and he had done a lot of growing since then.

"Declan," Cillian breathed. "What the feck are you doing in America?" Cillian and Lilly were the only ones to make the move to America. The rest of the family stayed in Ireland, even after their parents passed away.

"I'm looking for Lil," Declan said. "I need to talk to her about some trouble that might be coming her way."

"What kind of trouble?" a woman asked from behind him. He turned to find his little sister standing there with her hands on her hips, just like their ma used to do when she was questioning one of them. She looked just like their ma too. Declan pulled her into his arms and squeezed the crap out of her.

"I thought you might be dead until they came looking for you," he said. He hadn't heard a word from her or Cillian since she arrived in America over a year ago, and he feared the worst.

"You're squeezing the life out of me," she breathed. "Put me down, Declan." She was always a bossy little thing. Even when they were kids. Lil might have been the youngest, but she was usually in charge.

He dropped her from his arms, letting her feet hit the floor with a thud. "Sorry, Sis," he said. "I'm just so happy to see you in the flesh. The Dead Rabbits told me that you were alive in America, but that was all they knew."

"Fuck," Lil spat. She always had a filthy mouth. "The Dead Rabbits found you?"

"Yeah, they came around asking me questions and when I didn't have any answers for them, they beat the shit out of me. I was just happy to learn that you were alive and well, here in the states."

"I'm sorry that they did that to you," she said. "Are you all right?"

"I'll live, and you have nothing to be sorry about," Declan said. "You didn't tell them to beat the hell out of me."

His brother pulled him into a quick hug and released him. "You got big, little brother."

"Yeah, that's what happens when you grow up. The last time I saw you, I was about ten," Declan reminded. He hated that Cillian had decided to stay in America when the rest of his family returned back home to Ireland. Actually, he was pissed that his parents allowed their oldest son to stay behind. It only led to heartache for them both after Cillian went down the wrong path after being left up to his own devices.

"I'd say about ten," Cillian agreed. "You grew up good, brother," he said.

"Thanks," Declan said, "you look good too."

"Marriage and a bunch of kids grounded me," Cillian shared. "You'll have to come by and meet the family. How careful were you on your trip over?" Cillian asked.

"You mean to ask if I was followed," Declan guessed.

"Right, but I didn't want to make you sound like you couldn't handle yourself," Cillian said.

"I don't think I was followed, but the Dead Rabbits have men everywhere," Declan said. "I can't be certain."

"Doesn't matter," Lil insisted. "If they followed you here, they'll be sorry. Between my club and yours, we'll be just fine."

"Wait—you have a club?" he asked Lil. "What does that even mean?" He knew that walking into a biker club, it had to belong to someone, but he never guessed that it would be Lil's.

"I have an all-women's MC called the Royal Harlots and Savage has been good enough to let us meet here until we can get our own clubhouse."

"And Savage runs the Royal Bastards, and this is his place," Cillian said. "He's in the back room, but I'm sure he's going to want to see you," Declan remembered the big guy who had promised his parents that he'd keep Cillian out of trouble. Honestly, Declan hated him most of all for breaking his promise to them.

"I'm not sure that I want to see him," Declan mumbled under his breath. "He let us all down."

"If you're talking about me going to prison, then it's me you should be angry with. I was the fool who got involved with the gang that led me to steal cars. I was the one who made the decision to fall in with the wrong people. Savage tried like hell to get me back on the right path, but I was a fool-hearted kid who didn't know any better. Savage was there to pick up the pieces when I got out and get me back on my feet. It's because of him that I met my wife, Viv."

"I'm sorry," Declan said, "I didn't know any of that."

"How could you?" Cillian asked. "I was too prideful to reach out to everyone back home to share my story. I should have done so, but I was too ashamed of what I had done."

"You served your time, and you got out," Declan reminded. "You made something of yourself and Da and Ma would be so proud to know that you've made them grandparents." Some of their brothers and sisters back in Ireland had kids, but his parents would have been so happy to know that Cillian had changed his life for the better and now, had kids of his own. "I can't wait to meet your family."

"Good, because you'll be staying with us," Cillian said.

"Is that safe?" Lil asked. "If the Dead Rabbits followed him here, your family would be in danger."

"I'll take precautions," Cillian assured.

"No, you won't because I'm not staying with you," Declan said. "Lil is right, I can't be sure that I wasn't followed, and I won't put your family in danger." Lil opened her mouth to speak, and Declan held up his hand, stopping her. "And before you invite me to stay with you, I won't. I can find my own place to lay low."

"Actually, I was going to say that Savage has a few apartments over the bar here, and I'm sure that he'll let you stay in one of them," Lil said. "Cian and I stayed in one for a few months until we could get a place of our own."

"Cian, as in the boy who followed you around town like a puppy? Let me guess, he's followed you here too?" he asked.

"Yes, that Cian, and now, he's my husband, so be careful about what you say next," Lil warned.

"Are you happy, Lil?" Declan asked.

"I am," she said, defiantly raising her chin as if challenging him to question her. He wasn't about to do that.

"Then, I'm happy for you," he said. "Congratulations, Lil," he said, pulling her in for a quick hug. "How about you find out if Savage is available, Cillian, and I'll speak to him about staying here." It wasn't going to be forever, and Lil was right, he couldn't put any of his family in danger if he had led the Dead Rabbits to Savage Hell.

"Be back in a sec," Cillian said.

"I have to talk to Savage too. Will you be good here for a few minutes?" Lil asked.

"I'm not a child," Declan insisted. "I'll grab a beer at the bar and wait for you both to return."

"Sounds good," Lil said, following Cillian to the back of the bar.

Declan made his way to the bar and sat down on one of the empty stools. "Beer please," he said to the woman behind the bar. She smiled at him and nodded, pouring him a beer.

"We only have one kind on tap here," she said, "Sorry."

"It's fine," he said.

"Hey, you're not from here," she noted.

"What gave it away?" Declan asked.

"Well, you sound like our Prez, Lil, so I'm guessing that you're from Ireland like her?"

"I am," he agreed, "in fact, I'm her older brother, Declan James."

"Good to meet you," the woman said. "I'm Angel Desoto, but you can call me Sprite."

"Sprite?" he asked.

"Yeah, it's my biker's name. It's a long story, and well, we're kind of busy right now, but I'd be happy to tell you about it later when I'm on my break." The last thing Declan was looking for was a woman, but he supposed a quick roll in the hay might be just what he needed after a long trip. What could it hurt?

"He'd love to, but he already has plans," a woman said from behind him. She didn't sound American. In fact, she sounded English, and getting involved with an English she-devil wasn't going to happen.

"I'm sorry," he said, turning on the barstool to find the

sexiest blond he had ever seen standing behind him. She was wearing a skintight sweater and jeans that made his mouth water. "Who are you?" he asked.

The woman pulled a gun from her purse and nudged it into his side. "I'm someone you're going to want to talk with," she whispered into his ear.

Declan didn't want to cause any trouble, and the woman pushing her gun into his side was definitely trouble. "Um, sorry, Sprite," he breathed, "but, she's right." He downed his beer and threw down a twenty. "Have a good night." He stood and left the bar with the sexy blond, hoping like hell that someone would report back to his brother and sister that he had left with her. Hopefully, they'd put two and two together and come up with the fact that Declan was in over his head and needed help —before it was too late.

DANGER

Bernadette Danger wasn't about to give up chasing down every lead to her brother, and the big Irish bloke standing next to her was a major lead. Of course, her snooping was "Unofficial" since MI6 wouldn't sanction her going rogue looking for Anthony, but she couldn't let him go. He was her little brother and her only living family.

"You want to tell me why you've got a gun shoved into my side?" the sexy Irishman asked.

"Because I need to talk to you, Mr. James," she said.

"Well, that doesn't seem very fair," he said. "You seem to know my name, but I have no idea what yours is."

"Bernadette Danger," she said without pause, "but, you can call me Danger."

He barked out his laugh and she stopped to look him over, trying to figure out what was so funny. "Fitting," he said. "Your name is very fitting for you, Ms. Danger."

"It's not Ms. Danger, just Danger," she insisted. The guys in her graduating class had dubbed her last name as her moniker and they felt the same way about her nickname. Danger seemed to find her wherever she was and now, it had caught up to her brother, Anthony.

"Okay then, Danger," he said, "what can I do for you?"

"You can help me find my brother," she blurted out. She had planned on waiting for a more private setting than a parking lot at a dive biker bar, but here she was, spilling her guts.

"I'm not sure that I follow," Mr. James said. "Who is your brother? Do I know him?"

"No," she breathed, "but, you know the people who have taken them. I've been watching the Dead Rabbits for months now, trying to get any intel on Anthony, and you seem to have quite a relationship with them, Mr. James," she said.

"I have nothing to do with those assholes," he spat. "In fact, I had to come here just to get away from them. They did this to me as a parting gift." He pointed to the bruises on his left cheek and his swollen right eye.

"They beat you up?" she asked. Bernadette was sure that he was a part of the Rabbits with the way they kept going around his place.

"They did and promised to keep coming back until I gave up where my sister was living," he admitted. "So, I packed my bags and headed here, to warn her that the Dead Rabbits are looking for her and her apparent new husband."

"You mean, your sister is in there?" she said, nodding back to the bar. Lilianna James was one of the people of interest at MI6 and she might be able to get some information about Anthony if she got to talk to her. "Would she be willing to speak with me?"

Mr. James barked out his laugh, "If you're willing to leave

your gun in your purse, I'm sure that Lil will talk to you. She's kind of strong-willed and won't take as kindly to you poking a gun into her side as I have."

"Would you have talked to me otherwise?" she asked.

He shrugged, "Sure," he offered. "I'd talk to anyone, but you made it very clear that I didn't have a choice." Bernadette knew that she might be playing her hand all wrong, but she needed his help and if she could get his sister to help her too, then she was sure that she'd find Anthony. All she could do was go on faith and with a little luck, she'd get her way.

She shoved her gun back into her purse and took a deep breath, expecting the worst. "How about now?" she asked. "Are you still willing to speak with me, Mr. James?" she asked.

"How about you buy me a beer and we'll see how things go. I can also introduce you to my sister if you're willing to come back into the bar with me," he said. She really had no other choice. Bernadette was at his mercy and if she wanted answers, she'd have to play by Mr. James's rules.

"I'd be delighted to buy you a beer," she breathed.

"Great," Mr. James said, "lead the way." Bernadette started for the bar, not bothering to look back to see if he was following her. All she could do now was hope that he'd coop-erate with her and answer some of her questions, otherwise, Anthony would be lost to her.

Bernadette sat in the middle of some very pissed-off-looking bikers and Lilianna James, who everyone called Banshee. She seemed to be the leader of the women who each sat next to their men. It didn't escape her notice that Declan James had no woman by his side.

"So, do you want to tell me why you dragged my brother out of here at gunpoint?" Lil asked.

"I'll admit that wasn't my finest decision, but you have to understand that I'm desperate to gain any information that might help me find my brother. He's all that I have left in the world," Bernadette whispered.

"As we've explained, none of us are a part of the Dead Rabbits," Cillian James reminded.

"Yes, you've said, but you have each had run-ins with them and I was hoping that you might have some intel as to where they might be based here in Huntsville. I've heard that they might be holding him here in town," she said. Before taking a leave of absence from MI6, she found out that Anthony might have been transported to Alabama and she knew that she had to try to find him. She even tried to persuade her boss to let her take a team to the States to search for Anthony, but he refused. He told her that finding her brother wasn't MI6 business, and she knew that arguing with him would get her nowhere. Her boss wasn't one to break or even bend the rules.

"I can ask around if it helps," Lil offered. "My husband, Cian, worked for them for a while. That's how I got mixed up with them. When he walked away from the Dead Rabbits, they threatened me, just like they did Declan. We need to stop them from coming for our family. Would you be willing to help us with that, Danger?" Lil asked.

"What makes you think that I'd be able to help you with the Dead Rabbits?" Bernadette asked. "If I could do that, don't you think that I'd find my brother on my own?"

Lil shrugged, "Maybe, but I have a feeling that you're more self-reliant than you've been letting on. I mean, you've got a gun in your purse to prove my point." Shit, the last thing she needed was to have to admit that she was MI6. This wasn't even official business.

"If I had to guess," Cillian said, "I'd bet that you were MI6, but that begs the question as to why you'd need our help," he said. "I mean, can't MI6 handle something as simple as a missing person?"

"I'm sure that MI6 is quite capable of handling a missing person case, but finding Anthony is something that I'm doing on my own," she admitted.

"So then, you admit that you're MI6," Declan almost shouted.

"Keep your voice down," Bernadette spat, "I'm not here on official business." She stood and threw down a wad of cash to cover their bar tab. "This was a mistake," she said, "I'm sorry to have taken up so much of your time." She turned to leave, and Declan grabbed her arm.

"We'll help you," he said. She wasn't sure if she should be relieved or worried that his help was going to come with strings.

"At what cost?" she whispered.

"At the cost of total honesty. You need to be one hundred percent truthful with us, and we'll do the same with you. That's the only way that we'll get close enough to the Dead Rabbits to find out if they have your brother. Do we have a deal?" he asked, holding out his hand to her. She looked it over as though it offended her in some way and sighed.

"We have a deal," she agreed, shaking his hand. Bernadette was sure that she was going to come to regret agreeing to his terms, but Declan James and his family were all the help she had, and God help her, she needed them.

What's coming next from K.L. Ramsey? You won't want to miss the second book in the new Dirty Riders MC Series-Riding Shotgun, is coming in January 2024!

MELODY

Melody Newton didn't really know her self-worth. She was never taught to stand up for herself and she had the bruises to prove it. But now, she was going to get a crash course in what it meant to stand her ground and give a damn about herself. Now, she was going to finally tell her good-for-nothing husband to hit the road. She had caught him sneaking around on her again, and this time, she had no forgiveness left to give him.

Adam walked into the kitchen and kissed her cheek, just as he always did before dinner. That was when she'd make a fuss about asking him how his day was and tell him about what she and their two-year-old daughter, June, did together while he was supposedly at work. But that wasn't going to happen tonight because she knew where he had been all day. Adam had spent all afternoon at the sleazy motel on the outskirts of town with some whore he probably had picked up a disease from. Melody knew this bit of information because her loving husband had used his credit card to pay for both as if he just didn't give a fuck about her finding out what he was doing—or in this case, who.

"How was your day?" he asked.

"My day?" she questioned. "Well, my day was very exciting. You see, I took June to the grocery store to pick up some groceries," she started.

"Yeah, I was going to ask what was happening with dinner. You haven't even started it yet? And where is our daughter?" June was usually sitting in her highchair, anxiously waiting for dinner, but Melody had gotten her sister, Tilly, to babysit June for the evening, so that she could face down her soon-to-be ex-husband. That's how Melody was getting through any of this right now. She just kept thinking that Adam would be her ex-husband, and she'd be able to start her life all over again. This time, she'd go it alone because there was no way that she'd allow another man to lay one finger on her ever again.

"Tilly took June for me," she said. "And dinner isn't ready, and it's not going to be ready, because my credit card was declined at the store. We're over our limit."

"Well, shit," he grumbled, pulling a beer from the fridge and popping off the top. "I'll put some money in the bank in the morning." She watched as Adam took a long swig of his beer and slammed the bottle down to the kitchen table, causing her to jump. "Since your sister has June, what do you say you and I have a little bit of fun, and then I'll take you out for a burger." The thought of Adam laying one finger on her repulsed her. He still smelled like the cheap hooker that he had spent the whole afternoon fucking.

"No thank you," she breathed.

"What do you mean by, 'No thank you?'" he asked.

"I mean that I don't want to have any fun with you, ever again, Adam. It means that I know why my credit card was over the limit and I couldn't buy food for our daughter. You used my card to pay for a whore and a motel room, didn't you?" she spat.

"You watch your fucking mouth, Melody. I told you that I wasn't going to do that again, and I haven't," he said, keeping up with his lie. If given the chance, Adam would rather die than claim the truth. But she knew the truth, even if he wouldn't say it out loud. He had cheated on her before, with her best friend from high school. Yeah, that one hurt like a bitch, but she forgave him. Melody was six months pregnant and a fool for thinking that staying with Adam was better for her and her unborn child than leaving him. She should have gotten out then, but she was too afraid to make a move that would cost her the roof over her head, so she stayed, and things went from bad to worse.

After he swore that he'd give up cheating on her, he got angry. It was as if he blamed her for not allowing him to screw around. Adam started getting rough with her and after a few times pushing her around and shouting at her, he finally hit her. She took it too, not wanting to cause waves. A part of her believed that she was responsible for his anger. She could deal with his anger, it was his cheating that broke her heart, so she stayed.

But now, finding out that he had cheated again, she felt numb. Melody was ready to walk out. Her and June's bags were packed and in the trunk of her car. Tilly said that they could stay with her and her new husband, Owen, for a while until she could get back on her feet. She had a plan and for the first time in her life, Melody felt like she had some self-worth.

She defiantly raised her chin to Adam as if daring him to hit her. "You did cheat on me, Adam," she insisted. "I have the credit card records to prove it. You've been going to that motel again, and this time, you've been paying for whores. Did you really believe that I wouldn't find the charges?" she asked.

"Maybe I just didn't fucking care if you found them," he spat. Adam sucked down the rest of his beer and grabbed another one from the fridge. If he continued drinking at this pace, she only had a small window of opportunity to let him know that they were done.

"I want a divorce," she said, cutting right to the chase.

"Well, that's just too fucking bad," he shouted. "You and I are married, for better or worse, and you're not leaving me."

"I am leaving you and I'm taking June with me. I want a divorce and I'm going to go to a lawyer tomorrow. I'm sure that my credit card records will be enough to prove that you've been cheating on me." He put the new bottle of beer on the table and stepped closer to her. He smelled like cheap perfume and pussy. God, it made her want to gag, but she held it back. There was no way that she'd show any weakness around him ever again. She had already done enough of that to last a lifetime.

She stared him down and when he smiled and turned away, she thought that he was going to pick up his beer and leave her alone, but she was wrong. Adam quickly turned back and punched her so hard in the face that she landed on her ass, and damn if she didn't see stars.

"You feel better?" she slurred. She was sure that her eye would swell shut in a matter of minutes and he was only getting started—that she knew from experience.

"Not yet, but I plan on hitting you until I do," he growled.

"That's usually your plan, asshole," she said, sitting up from the kitchen floor. He stood over her and she smiled up at him, knowing something that he didn't gave her a second wind.

"Why the fuck are you smiling at me, bitch?" he spat.

"Because for the first time, in a damn long time, I think I'm actually going to win this one," she said.

"You think that you can beat me?" he asked. Adam clenched his fist, an act that usually made her cringe, but this time she didn't feel anything. She had an ace up her sleeve—a large biker who stood in the doorway to her kitchen, and damn if he didn't look pissed off enough to tear Adam limb from limb.

"She might not be able to beat you, but I'm pretty sure that I can," Maverick growled. God, he was her knight coming to save her and she'd take it, even if she had just mentally sworn off all men forever.

"Who the fuck are you?" Adam shouted, turning his back on her. That's how he treated her—always underestimating Melody and thinking that she'd never retaliate. She was ready to take her stand, and when she found her feet, grabbing the frying pan from the stove top, she swung it at the back of Adam's head, knocking him out. He fell to the kitchen floor with a thud, and she tossed the frying pan to the ground.

"Hey, Maverick," she breathed, "can you call the police for me? I need to make sure that I didn't just kill my soon-to-be ex-husband."

He shook his head at her and smiled. "I knew that I liked you, kid," he said, calling her by that annoying little nickname he used for her. Melody knelt down to find that Adam still had a pulse. She stood, not sure if that was a good or bad thing. One thing was for sure, he wouldn't let her retaliation go unpunished and there was no way that he'd underestimate her again.

MAVERICK

Maverick Blaine knew something was up when he showed up at his brother's house and found him and his new bride babysitting Melody's kid. As soon as he walked into their house, the toddler made a beeline for him and begged to be picked up. He didn't mind kids, really, and Melody's brat was the cutest one he knew. He asked her where her mama was, and she just smiled back at him, giving him that blank stare that she usually gave him as she checked him out. June was fascinated by his beard and tats. He just wished her mom felt the same way about him, but Melody was a married woman, and he wouldn't cross that line, no matter how badly he wanted to.

Mav asked Tilly where Melody was, and she told him that her sister had some things to work out with her husband. That was all he got from her before she took June from him and whisked her off to the bathroom for a bath. It wasn't until he found his brother sitting in the kitchen, drinking a beer, that he got a straight answer about what was going on. That was when Owen told him that Melody had caught her scumbag husband cheating on her, again. He couldn't believe that anyone would cheat on her once, let alone twice. Hell, the woman he knew was sassy and confident and would never let some loser cheat on her.

Owen went on to tell him that he thought that letting Melody go back to her house to face her husband alone was a bad idea. He said that the asshole liked to smack Melody around and that's when Maverick lost it. He questioned his brother for letting Melody face that jerk alone and then stormed out of the house, mumbling something about needing to beat his little brother's ass.

He was right to show up at Melody's house unannounced too. When he got there, he snuck into the back kitchen door and found her husband standing over her, shouting that he was going to beat the shit out of her. And from the looks of Melody, who was already lying on the floor, he had already started. It took all his restraint not to run in and pummel the guy. And when Melody stood and hit the fucker in the back of the head with a frying pan, he felt a sense of pride that he had no right to feel about her. She was one tough chick and had had the physical and mental scars to prove it.

He called the police, and they showed up at her house, taking Melody's statement and arresting her husband for abuse. Maverick corroborated her statement, telling the cops that she acted in self-defense, and how he had found her on the floor after her husband had hit her. Mav's only regret was that Melody didn't kill the fucker. He was going to be taken to the hospital, to get checked out, and then, they were going to hold him until his bail hearing. He'd get out and then, he'd probably go after Melody and her kid, and Mav wouldn't let that happen. He just had to figure out how to convince her to let him take both her and June back to his place. Her ex would look for her at home first, and then, when he couldn't find her there, he'd head over to Tilly and Owen's place. His brother could handle the guy, but Mav didn't want Melody or June to have to go through any of that shit. Her asshole ex didn't know where he lived and that would give them both a safe haven while Melody figured out her next move.

He watched as the last of the cops left and Melody looked around her kitchen. "What now?" she asked.

"Now, we get you out of here," he said.

"Oh, yeah," she breathed. "I forgot all about calling my sister. She must be worried to death about me."

"I called Owen and filled him in. June is asleep and safe," he said, knowing that would be her next question. The few times that he was around Melody and her kid, he could tell that she was a great mother. He just had no idea that she was dealing with an abusive asshole at home.

"Thank you for doing that," she said. "God, what am I going to tell June about her father?" she asked. He really didn't have any answers for her. His own father was an asshole, and his poor mother was constantly covering for him and his bad behavior. But he and his brothers knew the deal. His father was a jerk and when he happened to be around, things were awful. Mav knew how much his mother struggled when his father would take off. She worked two jobs to put a roof over his and Owen's head and food on the table. The thing was, he and Owen were so much happier when their old man was gone, and he had a feeling that June would feel the same way about her father not sticking around.

"When she's old enough, you'll tell her the truth. Tell her how her brave mother stood up to a man who liked to beat her up. Tell her how strong her mom is, but I'm sure she'll already know all about it."

"Thank you for saying that, Mav," she whispered, swiping at the tears that were running down her cheeks. "I'm sorry I'm crying. I guess it's just been a long day. I need to get over Tilly's. She's expecting me."

He grabbed her hand and she flinched, making him feel like a complete ass. Of course, she'd react to him that way. She had just had the shit beat out of her—Melody had the black eye to prove it. "I'm sorry," he said. "I'd never hurt you, Melody."

"I—I know that, Maverick. I'm just a little shaky is all. I didn't mean to react that way."

"I just wanted to talk to you about staying with Tilly and Owen," he said.

"Okay," she breathed, "is there a problem with me staying with them?"

"Not a problem," he said, "more like an issue. Owen is worried that after Adam gets out of jail, he'll come looking for you here."

"Right, and when he can't find me here, he'll search for me at Tilly and Owen's place. God, I'm an idiot. He doesn't want me there because he's worried that I'll put them in danger."

"No," Maverick said, "God, I'm screwing this all up. He's worried that he won't be able to protect you, Tilly, and June all by himself."

"Yeah, that makes sense," she said. "Um, I guess I'll just have to find another place for me and June to stay—you know until everything dies down with Adam." He didn't want to be the one to tell her that things might never die down with her soon-to-be ex. If he got out of jail, he might not ever leave her and June alone.

"How about you stay with me?" Maverick asked. She looked up at him as if he lost his mind, and maybe he had.

"That's not a good idea," she said. "I mean, won't I be putting you in danger then?"

He couldn't help laughing at the idea of him being put into danger by a mom and her kid staying with him. "I think that I'll be able to handle him if he shows up to my door."

"Yeah, you do seem capable," she said, looking him over. He liked the way that she took in every inch of him, letting her eyes roam his body. They had always had some unspoken connection, but he never acted on it knowing that she had a husband waiting for her at home. "But I don't want to put you out," she insisted.

"You wouldn't be putting me out at all," he assured. "I can keep you and June safe, I promise, Melody." He was making promises and getting involved—two things that he swore that he'd never do. But then again, Melody had him doing things he never thought he'd ever do, and with her, playing the protector, felt right.

Have you read the series that started it all? If not, what are you waiting for? You can pick up Book 1 of K.L. Ramsey's Royal Bastards: Huntsville Chapter- Savage Heat is available here -> https://books2read.com/u/brq7pA

And here's a special sneak peek at Savage Heat-Enjoy!!

SAVAGE

Savage watched as his latest failure floated down from the atmosphere back to earth. At least this time the damn parachute deployed, and he wouldn't have to start from scratch again to rebuild his rocket. Last time that happened, his boss threw a major fit, telling him to get his shit and clear out of his office. A short week later, his boss was standing on Savage's front porch, proverbial hat in hand, begging him to come back to work. He even gave him some bullshit about the government needing his service and all that shit. Savage didn't have the desire to tell his boss that he had not only served his government for almost twenty years, but he had also had the bullet holes and shrapnel in his leg to prove it.

Sure, he could sit around and complain about his past and wake up every day in pain, but where would that get him? It was his choice to join the Air Force and it was his choice to re-up when he could have gotten out. He saw active combat for the third time and that was when his copter went down and most of his buddies died. There was nothing he could have done differently that day but God, it was just about all he could think about every night when he laid down and tried to sleep. Their faces would flicker through his memories, and he knew that he was going to have another restless night ahead. It was who he had become since he was honorably discharged.

Of course, the Army was quick to jump on his specific skill set and make him the best fucking job offer he'd ever gotten. How could he refuse and why would he? He got to stay in Huntsville, Alabama, where his kid could stay in the same school with the only friends she had ever known. Uprooting Chloe wasn't part of his plan—the poor kid hadn't had much stability in her life. Chloe wasn't really his kid, but that wasn't something he liked to think about too often. It brought up too many bad memories and he tried to only look forward, never back.

Savage adopted Chloe when she was just six months old after her mother and father died in a horrible auto accident. She was his niece and when child services showed up at his doorstep with a baby in tow, claiming that his estranged sister had given him full custody in her will, what was he supposed to do? Savage didn't have one fucking idea how to take care of a kid and they were handing him one that still needed twenty-four-seven care. He quickly learned how to change a diaper and what to feed and not feed a six-month-old. Honestly, that last part was learned the hard way because the kid ended up not being able to handle table food at such an early age. Everything he fed her seemed to run through her like sand in a sieve. But that was all behind him now. He wasn't sure how he would have survived without that little girl. She had become his whole reason for living. Hell, she basically saved his life and gave him purpose and the will to keep going after his accident.

He had only been home for a few months when Chloe came into his life, and he was feeling pretty down and sorry for himself. Both of his parents were gone. His father was never really in the picture and his mom died the year he graduated from high school. Her death had sent him into a spiral that led to him joining the Air Force after he graduated. It also was one of the reasons his older sister, Cherry, stopped talking to him. She begged him not to go into the military; and even tried to guilt him into feeling bad about leaving her with no one, since both of their parents were gone. But he didn't listen. Hell, the only thing Savage wanted to do was ride his damn motorcycle and get the fuck out of that town. He was a punk-ass kid who didn't know any better and the day he left to enlist was the last time he saw Cherry alive.

Now, every time he looked at Chloe's sweet face, he saw his sister. He never met Chloe's dad, but he had heard that his sister met a good guy and got married. He liked to imagine Cherry happy with her beautiful new family, at least for a little while. She deserved some happiness after all the shit life had thrown at her, including a punk-ass, eighteen-year-old kid brother who thought he knew better than she did. God was he wrong. His relationship with Cherry was the one thing he regretted in life, but Savage learned that regrets would only hold him back and he couldn't allow that. He had too much going for him to wallow in self-pity.

"I think your rocket's a dud." Savage turned to find the hot guy who always seemed to follow him around Redstone Arsenal. It was as if the guy was his personal bodyguard with the way he watched Savage and he had to admit, he wouldn't mind having his body guarded by him.

"Yeah, well, this is literally rocket science, so I can't really use that old line." Savage looked the guy up and down, liking the way he filled out his fatigues. Not having to wear a uniform was one of the many perks of no longer being enlisted. He usually wore ratty old jeans and a t-shirt when he was on base, partially out of defiance but mostly for comfort. The Alabama heat was quite unbearable, but he was used to it. He never really lived anywhere else except for being stationed overseas.

"I'm Bowie Wolfe," the guy said, holding out his hand, waiting for Savage to take it.

He shook the younger guy's hand and smiled. "Are you named after the singer?" Savage questioned.

"Yeah," he breathed. "My mother was a huge fan and well, I got stuck with the name."

Savage shrugged, "All in all, I'd say you did all right. David Bowie is a legend, man," he said.

Bowie groaned and laughed. "Yeah, now you just sound like my mother," he teased.

"Thanks for that," Savage grumbled. He knew just by looking at the guy that he had a few years on him. Hell, he had more than a few years but that usually didn't bother him. Savage liked his guys young and feisty.

"Sorry, man. Um, I didn't catch your name," Bowie said.

"Savage," he offered.

"Wow—you gave me shit about my name but yours is pretty epic too. How did you get a name like Savage?" Bowie crossed his arms over his massive chest and waited him out. It wasn't something Savage liked to talk about, but the determination on the guy's face told him he really had no choice in the matter.

"Savage is actually my last name. My first name is Logan, but my club gave me the nickname after I told them about my helicopter going down. Lost a lot of good guys that day and my buddies said I'm still alive because I'm too savage to die."

"You served?" Bowie asked.

"Yeah—career Air Force until the accident and then honorably discharged," Savage admitted. "How about you?" Bowie held his arms wide as if showing Savage his fatigues to prove his point.

"I enlisted in the Army right from high school and haven't left yet. I've been in for twelve years now and I hope to make this my career, but we'll see." Savage did the math in his head and whistled.

"So, you're what—about thirty?" he questioned.

"I'll be thirty-one in a few months," Bowie admitted.

"You're just a kid," Savage teased.

"Yeah—okay, old man," Bowie said. Savage knew the guy was teasing but at forty-five, he was really beginning to feel his age. "And how old are you?" Savage winced at the mention of his age. It was something he usually didn't share because it wasn't anyone's damn business.

Savage smiled at Bowie, trying to deflect his question with one of his own. "Want to have a couple beers with me?" Savage knew he was pushing his luck with the younger guy, but he didn't give a shit. He was hot and tired, and Bowie turned him the fuck on. It was time to knock off and if Savage could convince him to have a couple of beers, then he might be able to talk Bowie into coming home with him for the night. If he was reading the signals correctly, his new friend was interested but he had been wrong in the past—so who knew?

"You asking me out, Savage?" Bowie questioned. Now it was

Savage's turn to waiver in his answer and he suddenly worried that he had misread the chemistry that hummed through the air between the two of them.

Savage shrugged, "Maybe I am," he said, not really answering Bowie's question. The guy was as stoic as they came and Savage was trying to read him, but he wasn't having any luck.

"Listen, if I misread the situation, then just forget I asked," Savage grumbled. He picked up the last part of his rocket that landed a few hundred feet away from where he had parked and by the time he turned around and headed back to his pick-up truck, he found Bowie leaning up against the passenger side door, his hands shoved deep into his pockets.

"I'm in," Bowie said, flashing him a wolfish grin.

"Sounds good," Savage said. He was trying for nonchalant, but his tone sounded anything but. It had been a damn long time since he met a man who made his cock pay attention, but Bowie did that for him. Savage needed to get himself under control or he'd blow his whole cool guy routine. Hell, he was far from being cool, but Bowie seemed interested, and he wasn't about to do anything to fuck that up.

"You have someplace in mind?" Bowie asked, helping Savage shove the last of his equipment into the back of his pickup. "I mean, do you have a place you usually go to, you know, for a few beers?"

Savage liked the way Bowie seemed just as flustered about their situation as he was. He found it kind of cute the way the guy was floundering for words. He could have helped him out but giving him a hard time felt like the better option and would be a lot more fun.

"You mean, like a gay bar?" Savage asked. He knew he was

adding fuel to the fire, but he didn't care. Bowie turned an adorable shade of red that ran down his sexy neck and had Savage wanting to see just how far down his blush went.

"Well, I mean—sure. Or any bar, for that matter. It doesn't matter to me," Bowie stuttered.

Savage reached out and put his hand on Bowie's arm. "I'm just messing with you," he said. "I don't know of too many gay bars in Huntsville. I usually just go to my own bar, but I don't really advertise that I'm gay and I don't feel like answering questions tonight. You mind just going to the Voodoo Lounge? It's a bit yuppie but I think we can blend in with the regular crowd. Plus, they've got great live music a few nights of the week."

"Wait—you have a bar?" Bowie asked.

Savage smiled and nodded, "Yep—the bar's called Savage Hell. It's also where my motorcycle club meets. We're a part of the Royal Bastards, which is a nationwide MC, but my little chapter calls themselves Savage Hell, after the bar. I try to keep my personal and private lives separate."

"Meaning you haven't shared that you're gay with your club," Bowie guessed.

Savage wasn't sure what to say to Bowie's assessment. On the one hand, he felt the need to set him straight, and on the other, he wanted to tell him it wasn't anyone's business whom he was having sex with. From the way his body was responding to Bowie, he hoped to have sex with him before the end of the night.

"Listen," Savage said. "I learned a long time ago that who I'm fucking is no one's business. I like you, Bowie, but if you're not interested, tell me now if I'm wasting my time."

"I was just talking, man," Bowie said.

Savage sighed, "Yeah—I'm just on edge lately with these damn tests needing to be done yesterday and I'm being an ass. Sorry," he offered. "And to answer your question—I haven't told my club that I'm bi." Hell, he hadn't told many people about that part of his life. Savage was careful not to bring any of the men or women he slept with home to meet Chloe. He didn't want to expose his daughter to his unstable dating life and that was exactly what it was—chaotic.

He hadn't been much of a serial dater, usually not making it past one night with a person. It was easier that way. He didn't have to make any promises to anyone, and he didn't expect anything in return. The one time he broke his no-dating rule, he ended up running away like a fucking coward when messy feelings got in the way.

"So, we doing this?" Savage asked. He started for the driver's side of his pick-up, not waiting to see if Bowie was going to join him or not.

"I get it," Bowie said. "I don't share that part of my life easily. I haven't even come out to my family yet." Bowie slipped into the passenger side of the cab of the truck and pulled his seatbelt on, clicking it in place.

"What about your truck?" Savage asked, nodding to where Bowie's vehicle sat, just down the road.

"I'll get it tomorrow when I'm back on duty. That is if you don't mind giving me a lift back to my place later." Bowie seemed to assume Savage would just agree and honestly, he didn't mind. If he was Bowie's ride for the night, there was a better chance they'd end up in Bowie's bed for a little while. Savage never left Chloe overnight, but he had a sitter with her, and he knew that she'd agree to a few extra hours if he paid double.

"Sure," Savage said. "No problem."

"Thanks," Bowie said. "I have to admit, I could use a night out. It's been a shit show around base, and I could use the break."

"Yeah, I heard about the cutbacks, and I guess being down so many people makes for more work for the ones who are left." Savage knew some other guys on base from his club and they were all complaining about the changes to the budget and having to take on more hours for the same pay. His MC was made up of mostly military guys, both active and retired. But his guys came from all walks of life—he even had a few one-percenters who he was happy to help get their lives straightened out. He liked helping his guys and even took a few of them under his wing, as a sort of personal project.

"Yep, it sucks. But what am I gonna do? Uncle Sam owns me, and I go where he tells me," Bowie said.

"Where are you originally from?" Savage asked. He usually didn't get too chatty with his "dates" but there was something about Bowie that made him want to know more about the guy.

"Texas," Bowie said.

"You get homesick?" Savage questioned.

"Naw," Bowie admitted. "Like I said, I still haven't come out to my family, and keeping a secret like that weighs on a person. It's easier being away from home and not having to worry about watching my back or saying the wrong thing."

"I get that," Savage said. "I haven't exactly been forthcoming about my sexuality with my friends or family either." He had a few close buddies in his club that knew the truth and he trusted them not only with his secret but with his life.

"I'd like to blame my military background for all the secrecy, but that really isn't an issue anymore," Bowie said.

"Yeah, that wasn't the case when I enlisted." Savage had served under the, "Don't ask, don't tell," era and he had to admit, it had its pros and cons. Not having people diving too deep into his personal life was always a plus. He valued his privacy over everything else.

"You originally from Huntsville?" Bowie asked.

"Yeah," Savage said. "My family was from here, but they're all gone now. Well, everyone except Chloe and me." Savage mentally kicked himself for talking about his daughter. It wasn't something he did with complete strangers, and he was starting to worry that asking Bowie out might have been a bad choice. Sure, the guy was the sexiest man he had seen in a damn long time, but he was completely blowing his rules out the fucking window with Bowie, and that usually didn't end well for him.

"Who's Chloe?" Bowie asked as if he was able to read Savage's mind.

"My kid," Savage admitted.

"You have a daughter?" Bowie asked.

"She's six and I adopted her when she was a baby. Chloe is my sister's kid and when she and her husband died in a car accident, I took Chloe in."

"Wow," Bowie breathed. "I'm sorry about your sister and brother-in-law. But Chloe is lucky to have you, man."

Savage shrugged, "Thanks. And I'm the lucky one. She came into my life when I was in a dark place, and she gave me a purpose. She's a great kid."

"That makes sense," Bowie said. "She seems to have a pretty awesome dad."

BOWIE

Bowie wasn't sure how the hell he had ended up in the sexy stranger's pick-up agreeing to go for a few beers with him. He had been watching Savage for weeks now, not that he'd ever admit to it. Bowie had always been attracted to older men and Savage was his type, right down to his salt-and-pepper beard that made him want to give it a tug.

It had been a damn long time since he found anyone interesting enough to go out for a few beers with. When Savage first asked him out, he wasn't sure he had heard him correctly. He usually had a pretty good idea when a guy or woman, for that matter, was interested in him. But Savage didn't give him anything to go by. It was hard to get a read on the guy and that made Bowie want him even more. He always did like a challenge.

Honestly, dating men was kind of new to him. He wasn't lying when he told Savage that he hadn't come out to his family yet. It was one of the reasons why he jumped at the chance to be transferred to Huntsville from Texas when the opportunity arose. He hated that he was taking the coward's way out, but that was easier than admitting that he was bi. He was even beginning to avoid his weekly calls home to his parents because he got sick of dodging their questions about whether he had someone special in his life. Even if he had, he wouldn't be able to admit it because that would mean telling his parents who he was.

"You're awfully quiet," Savage said. "You having second thoughts?"

"About beer—never," Bowie teased. Savage shot him a smirk that told him he wasn't buying him using humor to hide from the question.

"You always a smart ass?" Savage asked.

"Most of the time," Bowie admitted. "I use humor to mask what I'm really feeling. My therapist says it's a way for me to hide my true self because I'm afraid that if people get to really know me, they won't like who I am." Bowie looked at Savage and almost made it through without busting up laughing. Savage looked about ready to pull to the side of the road and kick Bowie's ass out of his pick-up.

"Really, man," Savage grumbled. "I'm not sure if you're kidding or not." He shook his head at Bowie and smiled.

"Your face, man," Bowie said between fits of laughter.

"Yeah, yeah. Laugh it up," Savage griped. "Was any of that true?" The sad fact was it was all true, but Bowie wouldn't admit that to Savage on what could potentially be their first date.

"Naw," Bowie lied. "I just like yanking people's chains." Savage looked at him as if he was trying to decide if he wanted to believe him or not. He seemed like a smart guy and if he was telling the truth earlier, a literal rocket scientist. Bowie worried that Savage would be able to see right through his facade and that scared the hell out of him.

"I mean, I've been to a therapist, but that was to work a few things out after I got back from active duty," Bowie admitted. Giving the guy some truth might throw him off the scent. It would be best to get through the night together without Savage finding out just how messed up he really was. That was another one of his secrets he didn't share with anyone—well, besides his therapist.

"Yeah—happens to the best of us. The Air Force shoved my ass into therapy after I got shot down, not that it helped much." Bowie knew just how a tragedy like that could affect a guy. He watched his best friend die after their Humvee was attacked. It should have been him who was lying on the side of the road, bleeding out but instead, it was his best friend, Drew.

They pulled into one of Huntsville's dive bars famous for its customers being a little on the shady side. It was a perfect spot for two guys who didn't want to be seen out together, to grab a few beers. No one got into anyone else's business in places like the Voodoo Lounge and that was just the way they both seemed to want it. He knew that score—Savage didn't look like the type of guy who had long-term relationships and that was fine with Bowie. He wasn't sure where he'd be tomorrow and settling down with someone like Savage seemed like a pipe dream. He never let himself imagine his life with a man. Hell, he never imagined settling down with anyone, if he was being completely honest.

Savage parked his truck and cut the engine. "Listen, man," he sighed, "if you changed your mind about all of this, I'd get it."

Bowie smiled at Savage and reached across the center

console to take his hand. "You keep saying that, Savage. But I haven't changed my mind—about the beer or you. I'd like to hang out with you tonight, no pressure and no strings. You up for that?" Savage nodded and if Bowie wasn't mistaken, he could have sworn the big guy was blushing.

"I'd like that," he said. Savage grabbed his baseball cap from the back seat and covered his bald head, running his hand down his beard and Bowie couldn't seem to take his eyes off the guy. He was hot as fuck and Bowie was mesmerized by his every movement. He had been for weeks, following him around, watching him on base. Savage was big but carried himself with confidence and grace. He had a persona that screamed alpha and that alone turned Bowie completely the fuck on. He liked older men because the few he had been with usually insisted on being in charge in the bedroom. He wondered if Savage would be just as demanding, and the thought sent a shiver down his body.

"You good?" Savage asked. Bowie shook his head and smiled.

"No, but it's nothing a few beers won't fix," Bowie lied. He had a feeling it would take more than alcohol to right what had been bothering him. In fact, Bowie had a sneaky feeling it would take at least a night of taking orders from the sexy man sitting next to him to start feeling like himself again.

SAVAGE

Savage felt about ready to turn back around and leave just as soon as he saw his ex sitting at the bar with her girlfriends. Apparently, one of them was about to get hitched and Dallas was there to help her celebrate. At least, that was what he had gathered from the group of rowdy women.

"Shit," he grumbled and sat down next to Bowie. He looked down at the end of the bar to where Dallas mean-mugged him and had the nerve to laugh.

"I'd say 'shit' doesn't even begin to cover it judging from the way that blonde is scowling at you, man. What did you do?" Bowie asked. That really was a loaded question. It was more like what he didn't do, that was the problem. She was the only woman that Savage dated more than just a few times. Hell, she was the only person he had any kind of relationship with his entire adult life. And he fucked it completely up with her. He ghosted Dallas when he realized he wasn't going to be able to commit to her. She'd never be enough for him and how did he admit something like that to her? It was easier to just walk away from her and hope that Dallas would just forget about him. Her angry scowl told him that hadn't happened yet.

"We dated," Savage admitted. "About a year ago."

"Wow," Bowie whistled under his breath. "So, whatever you did to that woman must have been big, if she hasn't forgiven you in a year."

"I didn't ask for forgiveness," Savage growled. "And I'm not looking for it now."

"Well, I didn't have you pegged as the dating type," Bowie said. Savage held up two fingers to the bartender, signaling that he wanted a couple of beers. The bar really didn't offer much in the way of choices and he was one of the regulars, on nights after he had a rough day at work and didn't want to deal with his MC brothers asking him a million questions. At the Voodoo Lounge, he could just be himself and no one really bothered him.

The bartender brought them their beers and a bowl of pretzels that looked like they had been set out for a few weeks. "Hey, Savage," the bartender said.

"Mike." Savage nodded. "Start me a tab," he ordered.

"Sure thing," Mike agreed and nodded to Bowie.

"You new here?" he asked.

"Yeah," Bowie said. "New to the area, really. I'm at Redstone Arsenal." Mike grunted and Bowie smiled.

"Well, women around these parts seem to burst into flames around guys in uniform. Just watch yourself with the piranhas at the end of the bar. One of the chicks is getting married but they seem to be out for a good time. Just fair warning; unless you're looking for something like that." Mike looked between

Bowie and Savage as if trying to access what was going on between the two of them and Savage growled.

"Thanks, Mike," he barked, all but dismissing the guy. Bowie laughed again and he wondered what was so funny, but he had a feeling he wouldn't like Bowie's answer. So, he didn't bother asking.

"Are you always so grumbly?" Bowie accused.

"No," Savage quickly defended, shooting him a look that probably told him he was lying. Bowie held up his hands as if in defense.

"Okay, man," he said. "No need to bite my head off. If you want to go someplace else, we can. Hell, we can go back to my apartment. I have beer there." Bowie shot him a wolfish grin, making Savage smile.

"I'm good here," Savage lied. He could feel Dallas' eyes boring into the back of his head and he wasn't sure what the hell to do about her.

"Liar," Bowie challenged. "That sexy blonde has you squirming in your seat. It's hot, really—the thought of you with her. I just don't want to cause any trouble. Does she know?"

"Know what?" Savage asked, playing dumb.

Bowie sighed. "Does she know that you date guys?" he whispered.

"No," Savage breathed. He sucked down half his beer and shot a look across the bar to where Dallas was still giving him the stink-eye.

"You ghost her or something?" Bowie teased and Savaged winced. "Fuck, man," Bowie spat. "You didn't fucking ghost that hot woman sitting at the end of the bar?"

"I did and can you keep it down, man?" Savage said.

"I'm pretty sure she can't hear me over this God-awful

honky-tonk music and the ruckus her girlfriends are making. Why did you do it?" Bowie asked.

"Because she would never be enough for me," Savage admitted. It was the truest thing he had said to Bowie, and he worried that made him sound like an ass. "We had been on a few dates, and I really liked her, but then I realized that if I dated her—you know, just her—I'd be denying half of myself. You know what I mean?"

Bowie nodded like he understood exactly what Savage was talking about and he realized that he had just assumed the guy was gay.

"You like women too?" Savage asked.

"Yep," Bowie admitted." In fact, I haven't been with many men. It was easier to deny that part of who I was while I was living so close to home. I didn't start exploring that side of my sexuality until I was stationed here. I had been on a few dates with men, but not a lot. So, I do get what you're talking about, man."

Savage sat back in his barstool and waved the bartender back over. "We'll take two more and buy the ladies at the end of the bar another round on me," he said. Mike nodded and walked back down to where the loud group of women sat and when he announced that Savage wanted to buy them a round of drinks, they all squealed and cheered. Well, everyone except Dallas. She shot him a look that could stop most men dead in their tracks, but he wasn't most men.

Dallas stood from her stool and started toward them, and Bowie cursed. "Um, I'm pretty sure the shit is about to hit the fucking fan now, Savage," he said. Savage had a bad feeling that Bowie was right.

He held his breath, second-guessing every decision he had

made that day, right down to asking Bowie out and buying Dallas' friends a round of drinks. Yep, he was thoroughly fucked and all he wanted to do was get the hell out of there. Savage stood and threw down a hundred-dollar bill, knowing that would cover his tab, and smiled at Bowie.

"That offer to get a beer at your place still stand?" Savage asked.

Bowie smiled and nodded. "Sure," he said. "But, for the record, you're being a chicken." He looked across the bar to where Dallas was making her way across the crowded dance floor and sighed. Bowie was right but he didn't give a fuck. Better to leave as a chicken than face his ex's wrath.

"Yep," he breathed. "Ready?" He held out his hand for Bowie, knowing he might be sending not only Dallas but everyone who was currently watching the exchange between them, a clear sign that the two of them were together.

Bowie took his hand, and they made their way to the front of the bar. Just as Savage stepped out of the doorway and into the night, he looked back to find Dallas watching him; frozen to her spot with her mouth gaping wide open. Yeah, she had gotten the message, loud and clear—he was leaving the bar with Bowie and there would be no backtracking now. There would be nothing he could do to erase the hatred and pain that he saw in her beautiful eyes.

DALLAS

Dallas St. James just about fell off her damn barstool when Savage walked into The Voodoo Lounge with the handsome guy in fatigues. The two made quite a pair and she wasn't the only female in the bar to notice them. Every woman in her group seemed to sit up and take notice of the new conquests as soon as they walked in, even the bride-to-be.

She thought she'd never see Savage again and that was just fine with her. They had dated for about a month and then nothing—he seemed to vanish off the face of the earth. It was her fault really. She never pushed to know more about him than his first name and the fact that he used to be in the Air Force. He had mentioned that he was a scientist, but Dallas worried that if she pushed for him to tell her more, he'd bolt. It was ironic, really. He ended up changing her life forever and then ghosting her, never to be heard from again—or so she thought.

Dallas was determined to steer clear of Savage and whoever the guy was that came into the bar with him, but then he went too far and bought the bridal party a round of drinks. Was he trying to get her attention? If he was, it worked. By the time she got her nerve up, Savage and the guy got up to leave but what she saw next—it couldn't have been right. The bar was crowded, and she had to have seen the whole thing wrong because if she wasn't mistaken, they were holding hands when they left the bar.

She tried to rejoin her girlfriends, but she just wasn't in the mood to party after seeing Savage. He dredged up everything she had worked so hard to suppress—her anger, her fears and damn it, even her desires. How could she still want him like she did after the hell he'd put her through over the past year since he left her without a word? Sure, Savage didn't make her any pretty promises. She thought she meant more to him than just a fuck, but she was wrong. She had not only misjudged him but so many other things too.

Dallas bowed out for the rest of the night, not really in the mood for the strip club the girls were heading to next. All she could think about was getting back to her little apartment and shutting the world out until she could think straight again. Savage always seemed to have that effect on her—made her thoughts a little cloudy. Seeing him tonight just reminded her of the crazy, lust-filled month that they spent together, and she needed to put those thoughts and images out of her head. There would be no more remembering the man who controlled her body, mind, and soul. Savage threw her away and that was going to be the painful reminder she took home with her tonight. He didn't want her, and she'd do well to remember that.

Dallas climbed the two floors to her apartment and unlocked the door, letting herself in. "Hello," she whispered.

"Hey—did you have fun?" Her friend Eden poked her head around the corner and smiled. "I'm assuming that since you are home so early my answer is no, but I thought I'd be polite and ask."

Dallas made a face and Eden softly cursed. "You saw him, didn't you?" She asked. Her friend always was able to pick up things.

"How the hell did you figure that out?" Dallas grumbled.

"You make a face anytime his name is brought up. Listen, I've never met the guy, but you're going to have to get over this anger you're harboring towards him. If not for yourself then for Greer," Eden said.

Dallas sighed and nodded. Her friend was right—she owed it to both herself and her daughter to stop hating the man who had given her the greatest gift she ever had.

"I ran into him tonight at The Voodoo Lounge," Dallas admitted.

"Well, shit. That's not good. Did you talk to him?" Eden asked. Dallas could hear the question her friend was really asking her.

"Just go ahead and ask," Dallas said.

"Did you tell him about Greer?" Eden dramatically whispered.

Dallas shook her head. "No. I didn't even get the chance to talk to him. He was sitting across the bar with some really good-looking guy and by the time I tried to make it across the crowded dance floor, they bolted."

"Good," Eden said. "You don't owe him anything, Dallas. He used you and left you pregnant and alone. Hell, you didn't even know if that fucker was alive or dead. Telling him about Greer would be a huge mistake." Dallas wondered if her friend was right. For months after Savage cut off contact with her, she worried that he had been in some horrific accident and was hurt or worse—dead. It was silly really but believing some made-up tragic story was so much easier than knowing the truth. He just walked away from her, and that realization stung like a son-of-a-bitch. Eden was right about one thing—Savage used her and didn't even have the common decency to tell her it was over. He was a coward, and he showed his true colors tonight when he ran out of that bar again.

"Maybe you're right," Dallas said with a shrug.

"No maybe about it, girl. You've proven that you don't need his damn help with Greer. You're an awesome mom and your daughter will get everything she needs from you and well—me, her fabulous auntie."

Dallas giggled, "Thanks, fabulous auntie," she teased. "I needed to hear that tonight. It was just so strange, you know?"

"You mean seeing him again?" Eden asked.

"No—the way he left out of that bar. First, he took off like his pants were on fire and then, I could have sworn that he was holding hands with the hot guy he was with."

"What?" Eden questioned. "As in—they were there together, on a date?"

"Yeah, but that's crazy, right?" Dallas asked. Maybe she hadn't seen them correctly or she had just misread the situation.

"Well, that would explain why he ghosted you," Eden offered. "Maybe he realized he liked being with guys," she teased.

"Are you implying that I turned him gay?" Dallas mocked

upset and Eden giggled.

"That is one explanation," Eden joked, but Dallas found the whole topic less funny than her friend seemed to. Dallas had more at stake in all of this—she had more to lose and there would be no way she'd take chances with her daughter's happiness, not even for the sexiest man she had ever known. When Savage walked away from her, he didn't realize he was also leaving behind a little piece of himself that would remind Dallas, every day, of the time they had spent together. Her three-month-old daughter, Greer, was the spitting image of her father and the reason why she needed to work through her anger towards Savage. She owed her daughter at least that much.

Don't miss the rest of K.L.'s Royal Bastards! Here is the reading order for the Huntsville Chapter:

Savage Heat-> **https://books2read.com/u/brq7pA**

Whiskey Tango-> **https://books2read.com/u/bQdX6v**

Can't Fix Cupid-> **https://books2read.com/u/b6Kpj0**

Ratchet's Revenge-> **https://books2read.com/u/m0KB0l**

Patched for Christmas-> https://books2read.com/u/bWGQrM

Love at First Fight->**https://books2read.com/u/3kL87R**

Dizzy's Desire->**https://books2read.com/u/mBwxqp**

Possessing Demon->**https://books2read.com/u/mlLjMB**

Mistletoe and Mayhem-> **https://books2read.com/u/boy68Z**

Bullseye- Struck by Cupid's Arrow-> **https://books2read. com/u/bPNZ8l**

Legend-> **https://books2read.com/u/mBVrKM**

Spider-> **https://books2read.com/u/38nWA6**

Blade's Christmas Ride-> **https://books2read.com/u/bQeqdd**

ABOUT K.L. RAMSEY & BE KELLY

Romance Rebel fighting for
Happily Ever After!

K. L. Ramsey currently resides in West Virginia (Go Mountaineers!). In her spare time, she likes to read romance novels, go to WVU football games and attend book club (aka-drink wine) with girlfriends. K. L. enjoys writing Contemporary Romance, Erotic Romance, and Sexy Ménage! She loves to write strong, capable women and bossy, hot as hell alphas, who fall ass over tea kettle for them. And of course, her stories always have a happy ending. But wait—there's more!

Somewhere along the writing path, K.L. developed a love of ALL things paranormal (but has a special affinity for shifters <YUM!!>)!! She decided to take a chance and create another persona- BE Kelly- to bring you all of her yummy shifters, seers, and everything paranormal (plus a hefty dash of MC!).

K. L. RAMSEY'S SOCIAL MEDIA

Ramsey's Rebels - K.L. Ramsey's Readers Group
https://www.facebook.com/groups/ramseysrebels

KL Ramsey & BE Kelly's ARC Team
https://www.facebook.com/
groups/klramseyandbekellyarcteam

KL Ramsey and BE Kelly's Newsletter
https://mailchi.mp/4e73ed1b04b9/authorklramsey/

KL Ramsey and BE Kelly's Website
https://www.klramsey.com

facebook.com/kl.ramsey.58
instagram.com/itsprivate2
bookbub.com/profile/k-l-ramsey
twitter.com/KLRamsey5
amazon.com/K.L.-Ramsey/e/B0799P6JGJ

BE KELLY'S SOCIAL MEDIA

BE Kelly's Reader's group
https://www.facebook.com/groups/kellsangelsreadersgroup/

facebook.com/be.kelly.564

instagram.com/bekellyparanormalromanceauthor

twitter.com/BEKelly9

bookbub.com/profile/be-kelly

amazon.com/BE-Kelly/e/B081LLD38M

WORKS BY K. L. RAMSEY

The Relinquished Series Box Set

Love Times Infinity

Love's Patient Journey

Love's Design

Love's Promise

Harvest Ridge Series Box Set

Worth the Wait

The Christmas Wedding

Line of Fire

Torn Devotion

Fighting for Justice

Last First Kiss Series Box Set

Theirs to Keep

Theirs to Love

Theirs to Have

Theirs to Take

Second Chance Summer Series

True North

The Wrong Mister Right

Ties That Bind Series

Saving Valentine

Blurred Lines

Dirty Little Secrets

Ties That Bind Box Set

Taken Series

Double Bossed

Double Crossed

Double The Mistletoe

Double Down

Owned

His Secret Submissive

His Reluctant Submissive

His Cougar Submissive

His Nerdy Submissive

His Stubborn Submissive

Owned Series Boxset

Alphas in Uniform

Hellfire

Finding His Destiny

Guilty Until Proven Innocent

Royal Bastards MC

Savage Heat

Whiskey Tango

Can't Fix Cupid

Ratchet's Revenge

Patched for Christmas

Love at First Fight

Dizzy's Desire

Possessing Demon

Mistletoe and Mayhem

Bullseye- Struck by Cupid's Arrow

Legend

Spider

Blade's Christmas Ride

Savage Hell MC Series

Roadkill

REPOssession

Dirty Ryder

Hart's Desire

Axel's Grind

Razor's Edge

Trista's Truth

Thorne's Rose

Lone Star Rangers

Don't Mess With Texas

Sweet Adeline

Dash of Regret

Austin's Starlet

Ranger's Revenge

Heart of Stone

Smokey Bandits MC Series

Aces Wild

Queen of Hearts

Full House

King of Clubs

Joker's Wild

Betting on Blaze

Tirana Brothers (Social Rejects Syndicate

Llir

Altin

Veton

Tirana Brothers Boxset

Dirty Desire Series

Torrid

Clean Sweep

No Limits

Mountain Men Mercenary Series

Eagle Eye

Hacker

Widowmaker

Deadly Sins Syndicate (Mafia Series)

Pride

Envy

Greed

Lust

Wrath

Sloth

Gluttony

Deadly Sins Syndicate Boxset

Forgiven Series

Confession of a Sinner

Confessions of a Saint

Confessions of a Rebel

Chasing Serendipity Series

Kismet

Sealed With a Kiss Series

Kissable

Never Been Kissed

Garo Syndicate Trilogy

Edon

Bekim

Rovena

Garo Syndicate Boxset

Billionaire Boys Club

His Naughty Assistant

His Virgin Assistant

His Nerdy Assistant

His Curvy Assistant

His Bossy Assistant

His Rebellious Assistant

Billionaire Boys Club Six Book Boxset

Grumpy Mountain Men Series

Grizz

Jed

Axel

A Grumpy Mountain Man for Xmas

The Bridezilla Series

Happily Ever After- Almost

Picture Perfect

Haunted Honeymoon for One

Rope 'Em and Ride 'Em Series

Saddle Up

A Cowboy for Christmas

Summer Lovin' Series

Beach Rules

Making Waves

Endless Summer

The Bound Series

Bound by Her Mafia Bosses

Bound by His Mafia Princess

Dirty Riders MC Series

Riding Hard

Riding Dirty

Riding Steel

The Dirty Daddies Series

Doctor Daddy

Baby Daddy

A Princess for Daddy

A Daddy for Christmas

The Kink Club Series

Salacious

Insatiable

WORKS BY BE KELLY (K.L.'S ALTER EGO...)

Reckoning MC Seer Series

Reaper

Tank

Raven

Reckoning MC Series Box Set

Perdition MC Shifter Series

Ringer

Rios

Trace

Perdition 3 Book Box Set

Silver Wolf Shifter Series

Daddy Wolf's Little Seer

Daddy Wolf's Little Captive

Daddy Wolf's Little Star

Rogue Enforcers

Juno

Blaze

Elite Enforcers

A Very Rogue Christmas Novella

One Rogue Turn

Graystone Academy Series

Eden's Playground

Violet's Surrender

Holly's Hope (A Christmas Novella)

Renegades Shifter Series

Pandora's Promise

Kinsley's Pact

Leader of the Pack Series

Wren's Pack

Printed in Great Britain
by Amazon

37750507R00076